FELONY AT FRIPP'S GRAVEYARD

Edited by Twyla Beth Lambert

Cover design by Fresh Design

Cover illustrations by Moran Reudor

Print ISBN 978-1-945419-95-9

Ebook ISBN 978-1-945419-96-6

LCCN 2021942021

FELONY AT FRIPP'S GRAVEYARD

A FORENSICS 411 MYSTERY

WHITNEY SKEEN

FAWKES PRESS

Dedicated to Rusty (2008-2020), who rolled into our lives on a stretcher, with two broken legs and a happy tail. We'll meet again at the Rainbow Bridge, sweet boy!

HANNAH

SUNDAY

U*nconscionable* (adj.) shockingly unfair, unjust, not principled

WHEN I HEARD THE DOORBELL, and then Hank's traitorous voice, I huddled at the top of the stairs and listened.

What was he doing here? Had he come to sprinkle some coarse Himalayan salt on the gaping, festering wound that was our friendship?

At that point I hadn't selected a word of the day, but it would be something with a negative connotation... an adjective that really captured the essence of Hank Boyd—betrayer in the first degree.

"Can you give Hannah this?" Hank said. "It's from Mrs. McFarland."

Mrs. McFarland was Stacy's mom. Stacy was the missing girl that Hank's dog, Chaucer, found buried on Pelican Island over the summer. She called us heroes in the *Vista Point Voice* after we discovered her daughter's body. I'm not sure how heroic it is to tell the parent of a missing child that their kid isn't *just* missing. I certainly don't hold the surgeon who told us about my brother on a pedestal, but maybe you lower your threshold for heroism when your kid's been nowhere to be found for thirty-five years.

"Of course," Mom told Hank.

Then he went and said it!

"I'm really sorry about your son. That must've been awful."

Is there a good *way for a nine-year-old to die?*

"Oh? Hannah told you?"

"Um, yeah."

He mumbled because he knew it was a lie. I didn't tell him anything about Ben! He freaking invaded my privacy! Pried into my past. Googled the crap out of my family!

"Well, that's good news if she talked to you about it," Mom said. "She must really trust you."

I did trust *him. Which obviously was a sizeable error in judgment.*

"She took Ben's death extremely hard."

And what—Mom—you didn't?

"We all did. It was an accident, but Hannah blamed herself. She usually met Ben at his classroom, and they waited in front of the school for me to pick them up. That afternoon she was late. Hannah thought she could've done something to prevent it if she'd been there. She was broken for a long time."

I peeked around the corner and saw him nod. *What a phony! That personal stuff hadn't been in any of the news articles. In fact, why was Mom talking to him?*

"We moved here for a fresh start—to get away from the memories. We were so excited when she met you. You took her under your wing and eased the transition to a new place. You're the first friend she's had in years."

Jeez, why not just tell him about my breakdown, too?

"The kids back home didn't know how to relate to her after Ben's death. She missed a lot of school in fifth grade. When she finally returned, middle school had started, and the kids had moved on without her. She felt even more left-out and isolated. The depression got so bad we had to place her in the hospital."

I put my head in my hands as my brain exploded. *He's going* to think I'm crazy! Fourteen-year-olds don't differentiate between crazy *and mental health crisis!*

"It's a major breakthrough that she talked to you about Ben," Mom said. "She's lucky to have you."

"Please tell her I'm sorry," Hank said. "She'll know what I mean."

A lump formed in my throat.

"I will. See you soon, okay?" Mom closed the door, then yelled my name, not knowing I was just around the turn of the stairs. By then I was crying.

"What?" I groaned.

"What's wrong? You've been like this for days," she said, sitting down on the step next to me. "Hank was just here. He brought this card and told me to tell you he's sorry. Did you have a fight?"

I nodded.

"I sort of figured that after how you acted at the TV interview a couple of weeks ago. What did he do that's so bad? Something unforgiveable?"

I nodded.

Of course, it was unforgiveable.

Mom turned to me with a look of deep concern. "Did he *hurt* you?"

I nodded.

She stood up. "I'm going to kill him! What did he do?"

I shook my head.

She touched my shoulder. "Tell me. How did he hurt you?"

I snapped. "He investigated me like I was some cold case! I didn't tell him about Ben—he found out on his own by nosing around in my room. He read my fifth-grade yearbook and then Googled Ben!"

Mom let out a sigh. "Well, thank god. I thought he, um... did something horrible."

"He *did* do something horrible!"

"You said he *hurt* you. I thought he, you know… touched you or something."

I gawked at Mom.

"Gross!" I said. "He freaks out if you even *think* about his personal space! Chaucer is the only person allowed inside his force field."

"Chaucer? His dog?"

"Uh-huh."

Mom sat back down and patted my knee. "Well, I'm glad to hear he didn't"—she cleared her throat—"physically hurt you. And, while I understand that you feel betrayed that he went behind your back, don't you think it's better he knows what you've been through?"

I shook my head. "That is so very glass-half-full of you, Mom."

She stood again and grinned. "IKR."

Mom offered her hand and pulled me to a standing position.

"Please don't talk in text. It's creepy."

"I like Hank," Mom said, "even if he did lose you on an uninhabited island. And for those seconds that I thought he was a sex offender, I didn't want to believe it. I think you should give him another chance. Just let yourself be encouraged by his interest in your backstory. Don't focus on the snooping; focus on the feelings that prompted him to snoop. He cares."

I wiped the tears from my cheeks and nodded.

"Does he blink like that all the time?" Mom asked.

"You noticed? I thought maybe I was imagining it."

"No, he definitely has some sort of tic," Mom said. "Maybe Tourette's."

"What's that?"

"One of my college roomates had it. She would clear her throat repeatedly when she was trying to fall asleep at night. I think it's more common in boys than girls, but she had it. I had to sleep with ear plugs, which ended up being good practice for dealing with your father's snoring."

"I wonder if the kids at school have noticed his blinking?"

"It's pretty hard to miss. I guess you'll find out tomorrow."

I wrinkled my nose. "Yeah... the first day of school. Can't wait."

"Well, you already have one good friend, if you can look past his mistake. Plus, there's the kids you met on the swim team this summer. And with all the news stories about you and Hank, you'll probably be signing autographs by this time tomorrow."

"Doubt it."

2

HANK
MONODAY

I n the United States, buses carry about 25 million kids to and from
school each day. On average, five children die each year in school-
provided transportation, which represents less than one percent of all
traffic fatalities nationwide. In fact, students are seventy percent more
likely to arrive at school safely taking the bus than if they ride in a car.
Because school buses are so large and heavily regulated by the government, deaths in bus accidents are usually the drivers of the other vehicles involved in the accident, not the bus passengers. For more
information on accidental deaths, see Forensics 411 episode 19, Ticket
to Die.

I STOOD at the intersection between my house and Hannah's,
thinking about her "word of the day" ritual. She was always
trying to expand her vocabulary. If she could read my mind,
she'd describe my current state as *trepidation*. I would say *dread*.
She'd flash me a smile and say, "That's why *one* of us is going to
win a Pulitzer Prize, and *one* of us isn't!"

But she hadn't spoken to me in weeks.

The festival of good vibes Mom had showered on me over
the previous week was well-intentioned but ineffective. In my

life, nothing good ever seemed to stick. Happy times, friends, even my father didn't linger. Hannah had proved to be a brief peak in my trough-laden life.

I tried some of my shrink's self-talk while I waited for the bus to come.

"It's a new year, a new school, a new bus. Maybe Dillon Buckley moved to some remote nation without internet or cell service. Your new haircut looks good. You've got a thousand followers, plus five hundred new subscribers to *Forensics 411*. You're the ninth most popular forensic blogger on the web. You're on your way to being a social media influencer!" I took a cleansing breath. "And you know what Dr. Blanchard said last time, 'Only *you* have the power to change your narrative!'"

That was my shrink's advice: *change my narrative.* He said that a new school was the perfect time for me to make a fresh start, but *I* needed to make it happen. If I waited for Dillon Buckley to change, I would be waiting a long time. It was up to me. *Yes. My mom paid a hundred sixty bucks an hour for that non-solution to my problems!*

The roar of the bus's diesel engine brought me out of my fantasy where Dillon had relocated to a land far, far away.

My same bus driver from middle school was back with her coffee breath and continuing battle with female pattern baldness. She seemed as unhappy to be there as I was. *Was every high school freshman as miserable as a school bus driver, or was it just me?*

I got on. Avoiding eye contact, I quickly pushed through the aisle and collapsed onto an empty seat about half-way back.

I searched the reflections in my window for Dillon's sandy blond hair, vacant yet feral eyes, and smug expression. According to what someone scratched into a cafeteria table in seventh grade, he had quite a pair of "soccer player legs," as well.

Whatever that meant.

I stole a glance toward the front of the bus where he'd had an assigned seat all the way through middle school. *Theoretically*, I suppose he deserved to start high school with a clean slate, but we all knew that wouldn't last long. He just couldn't help himself. He'd smart-mouth the bus driver sooner rather than later. The other kids on the bus would egg him on. His demonic tendencies would be affirmed—his leadership role among his peers, cemented.

After confirming that Dillon was not on the bus, I remembered his brother was an upperclassman and probably driving him to school. Since their family owned a car dealership, I pictured them in an obnoxiously loud muscle car, skidding into the school parking lot with music blaring like some bad teen movie. One, maybe both, would perch on the hood of their car as passersby paid tribute.

I sat back, exhaled, and relaxed. Most of my horrible middle school days had begun with an unpleasant—sometimes torturous—bus ride, courtesy of Dillon Buckley. Perhaps this year *would* be different.

Suddenly the driver slammed on the brakes and everyone, as dictated by their considerable immaturity, let out exaggerated groans.

The driver opened the doors, and Hannah scurried up the steps.

She was different. Her normally frizzy hair was straight and not spanning three time zones. Large block letters across her chest identified the maker of her shirt. *Was she wearing makeup?*

The metamorphosis had begun. She looked like one of *them*.

As Hannah surveyed the crowd, I lowered my eyes to spare us both. Rejection was worse when it came with eye contact.

I glanced up for a second while she floated through the narrow aisle, bumping kids' arms and backpacks as she made her way toward the back of the bus. She raised her hand above shoulder-height and moved it right, then left, then right again.

A wave?

"Can I sit here?" she asked, standing beside me.

"Um, sure," I answered, pulling my backpack off the seat.

After she sat, she said, "You know, in most western societies, when someone waves at you, you're supposed to wave back. Do we need to review that *again*?"

"Nope," I answered, smiling back. "I'm good."

She nodded. "Me, too."

We made small talk on the bus, mostly about our schedules, but inside I celebrated.

We didn't have any classes together, but that wasn't necessarily a bad thing.

3

HANNAH

E gocentric *(adj.) regarding the self as the center of all things*

HAVING SURVIVED the bus and homeroom, first period math was the next major obstacle to navigate. I spotted an empty seat next to a pretty girl with long, enviably straight hair. Mine was naturally curly and ultra-frizzy. Keeping its circumference smaller than Jupiter was a daily challenge involving deep-conditioning, a flat iron, and lots of product. For the first day of school, I had tamed the beast to near-perfection.

That well-proportioned, acne-free girl positioned herself in the middle of the classroom in a sea of empty seats. From the back of the room, I watched girls trickle in and flock to her like attentive forest creatures surrounding Snow White in nature's very own living room.

Any teenage girl with the most rudimentary understanding of the high school social hierarchy knew that *she* was the person to friend.

Her ladies in waiting carried themselves with the confidence of runway models, not the apologetic comportment of many fourteen-year-old girls who volleyed between wanting to be noticed and wishing they were invisible. They didn't have to rely on the color of their orthodontic rubber bands to draw the eye to their flawless faces. They let their clear complexions, compliant hair, and teen couture do the talking. Not a bad hair day among them.

Like a struggling nation gawking at the modernized world with envy, drooling over the telephone poles and paved roads, I slid into the throng of the obviously popular girls as if I belonged. It was a bold pre-emptive strike, but if I waited for an invitation, it might not ever come.

Finally, the pretty girl turned, surveyed me from head to toe, arched her eyebrows and said, "Who are you?"

"I'm Hannah Simmons. I moved here from Pittsburgh over the summer."

"I'm Madison Talbot. My father owns the McDiggle's. I get everything I want for free—so do my friends."

She turned around and called to Lexi Nguyen, a dark-haired girl I knew from the neighborhood's summer swim team. "Lexi, why are you sitting all the way over there? Come." She patted the empty desk in front of her.

Lexi scampered over and said, "Madison, I love those earrings!"

"Thanks, Lex." She touched them. "I picked them up at Blue Moon."

"No way!" Lexi said, "That's where I got this bracelet."

"Nice," Madison said with a giggle. "We should go shopping together some time." Then she turned back to me and folded a stick of gum into her mouth.

"Pittstown… that's in the mountains, right?"

"Pitts*burgh* is in Pennsylvania," I answered.

She chewed her gum robustly, as if it had societal implications that reached far beyond the walls of Vista Point High School.

"A Yankee, huh? Where do you live?"

"Bending Oak Drive."

"What's your father do for a living?" She cracked her gum.

"He's an attorney."

"Not one of those public defenders?" She wrinkled her nose as if she smelled the unwashed masses that populated a public defender's humble law office.

"No, he works at Patterson, Presler and Moore in Wilmington."

She nodded and shrugged one shoulder. "That'll do."

Madison cracked another small bubble between her teeth. "Bending Oak Drive?" She turned to Lexi. "That's in your neighborhood, isn't it? Doesn't Forensic Freak live there?"

"Boomer?" Lexi asked. "Yeah, he lives in the old part. My mom says someone needs to tear down his shack and build something nice like they did with that home for criminally insane kids."

That was my house she was talking about. Apparently, it had a long, storied past.

"That house wasn't a group home for the criminally insane; it had just been vacant a long time. My parents were the ones that bought it."

"Good job tearing that dump down," Madison said. "We need more people like your parents in this town."

"Thanks." Feeling confident, I added, "And Boomer goes by Hank now."

Madison gave me a silent dressing-down with her eyes then laughed melodramatically.

"Oh, my god! You're *friends* with Forensic Freak?"

Lexi piped in. "He's totally weird!" She leaned toward me. "You know he's got that stupid web show, right?"

A strawberry blonde girl took the seat beside Madison. "Why would anyone like dead people? They're *so* boring," she said. "Boomer is such a creeper. I heard he's one of those necromancers!"

A wizard? She thought Hank was a wizard.

"What's a necromancer?" Lexi asked the strawberry blonde.

"It's somebody who does it with dead people!" the girl answered. She gave me the once-over and said, "I'm Madysen H. I spell mine M-A-D-Y-S-E-N."

I shook my head. "A necromancer isn't a person who—"

"Did you see what Dillon posted last week on Forensic Freak's home page?" Madison T asked.

"What screen name was he using?" Madysen H asked with a snort.

Madison T shook her head and laughed harder. "Corpse-Kitty. He cracks me up with all his screen names. He asked some stupid question about kidnappings, and The Freak went on and on about it. I guess when you don't have any friends, you've got lots of free time to answer stupid questions from fake followers."

The girls all laughed.

"I can just see him spastically blinking," Lexi said in a mocking voice, "'Gee, CorpseKitty, that's an excellent question!'"

I smiled slightly and nodded as if to agree.

I had seen that post. Hank had given CorpseKitty a well-thought-out answer to the kidnapping question. It probably *had* taken him hours to write, and I'm sure he was excited to do it. He loved anyone who showed an interest in forensics. The truth that Dillon Buckley was CorpseKitty would crush him as much as when I'd told him that AutopsyAl was actually Dillon.

Were any of Hank's followers real people?

As the girls' giggles subsided, Madison T blew a bubble.

"OMG! I know where I've seen you!" She pointed at me then addressed the other girls. "She's the frizzy-haired girl from the newspaper that was working with Freak!"

"Her hair's not frizzy now," Lexi stated with a blank expression, still clearly unaware of our swim team connection.

Madison T snarled at me. "Look, *Nancy Drew*, it's *your* fault

Dillon's grandfather and great-uncle lost their jobs! You know they might go to jail! You made a big mistake getting mixed up with Boomer Boyd!"

I thought that when people recognized me as the girl who helped crack the Stacy McFarland case over the summer, they would consider me a hero. I certainly hadn't expected them to think I was the bad guy. How could anyone possibly think that Hank and I had done something wrong? We only uncovered the crimes that the mayor and police chief committed. We were "hometown heroes"—the hosts of WBCH-TV had said so in front of the entire tri-county viewing audience.

As Madison T verbally assaulted me, I melted silently into my desk, knowing that my one and only opportunity to breach the ranks of popularity had failed spectacularly and irreversibly.

Choking back my emotions, I recalled the advice Mom gave me that morning as I left for school: "Be nice to *everyone,* and you'll figure out where you fit. Be yourself, and you'll be great."

I scanned the room, searching for an escape route. An empty seat next to Katelyn Calhoun, who'd also been on the neighborhood swim team, beckoned me.

I grabbed my backpack and said, "I have trouble seeing the board. I'm just going to move up to the front."

Scurrying away like the rodent they thought I was, I heard Madison T smack her lips and say, "That little witch! Wait 'til Dillon hears about this!"

"Can I sit here?" I asked Katelyn.

"Sure," she answered, glancing back at Madison and her cohorts. "Diva issues?"

I shrugged and rolled my eyes.

"Look," Katelyn said. "You can't really blame the Madisons for their snark—especially Madison T. She has to balance popularity, cheerleading practice, and a boyfriend while maintaining a clear complexion and keeping her roots touched up. It's a lot of responsibility."

"Is it true what they said about Hank—that everyone makes fun of him?"

She seemed confused. "Who's Hank?"

"Hank Boyd. You guys know each other, don't you? He said your mom and his mom were old friends."

"You mean *Boomer*?"

"He goes by Hank now."

"Oh, that's right. I heard the teacher call him that in homeroom. I didn't realize he'd gone through identity reassignment, but I guess I don't blame him. Everyone wants a fresh start in high school." She nodded toward the Madisons. "You just never know whether *they'll* let you have it or not."

4

HANK

In 2014, the Centers for Disease Control and Department of Education released a joint report on bullying. They defined bullying as "unwanted aggressive behavior with an observed or perceived power imbalance." For decades, researchers hypothesized that low self-esteem caused certain people to bully. However, today's evidence shows that bullies bully others because they are narcissistic, have a sense of entitlement, or a disregard for other's feelings, not low self-esteem. For more details, see Forensics 411 *episode 46, "Bully for You."*

AFTER HANNAH HEADED TO HOMEROOM, I opened my folder to a map of the school. I didn't attend freshmen orientation because way too much of life was conducted in alphabetical order. Boyd and Buckley were uncomfortably close to each other. Going to orientation would've given Dillon the chance to turn all the kids with last names A through M against me before school even started. He had an incredible talent for manipulating people's worst inclinations into equally deplorable actions. It was his gift.

I'd highlighted all my class locations for quick reference, so I wouldn't look like a freshman.

I heard the sarcastic "oops" before I hit the floor.

"Did you go boom?"

I knew the jeering voice. And if my hearing ever failed, my nose would not. Each morning, he bathed himself in a vat of Ferocious cologne as if it were his very own pheromone, bottled for the pleasure of every teenage girl. The fumes he emitted typically warned me of his proximity, but that day he was down wind.

Dillon the Villain.

From the floor, I surveyed my surroundings. Dillon gawked above me—clearly not having relocated to Outer Mongolia or undergone significant personality changes over the summer.

I stood.

Two cronies flanked him, looking gleeful to be beginning a new year of battle in an unfamiliar theater with mysterious terrain to master; unaccustomed teachers to manipulate; novel subjects on which to cheat; ground-breaking homework to not do; and—though currently not indicated—new victims.

They should be bored with me by now.

"*Love* the new do," Dillon said with an effeminate tone and flamboyant brandishing of his wrist. "Sure hope you don't get gum stuck in it!" He laughed loudly and slapped his hand against his thigh. "Remember when that happened before? You had to get a buzz cut!"

Dillon had been the one to grind a wad of chewed bubble gum into the back of my head in second grade. I'd kept the buzz cut until this summer when I made a number of changes to my persona.

He glanced up to the second floor of the rotunda. "Say, where's your friend, 'Fro White?" That was one of his nicknames for Hannah.

I bent down to pick up my notebook, but Dillon beat me to it.

"Sorry, that's mine!" he said, with a smirk.

What it must be like to be unburdened by sociological mores!

"Oh, look!" Dillon said as he examined my highlighted

building map. "Here's a treasure map that tells us just where to find Forensic Freak every hour of the day." He nodded to his henchmen. "That's lucky for us!"

I stood up to my full height and glared at Dillon.

"That's not a map of my classes; it's a map of yours," I said. "Keep it, so you don't get lost!"

I pivoted with authority and marched down the hall, leaving Dillon and his posse speechless.

Under my breath I mumbled, "We're gonna call that *changing my narrative!*"

Granted, what I said made absolutely no sense whatsoever. It *was* a map of *my* classes, not his. Anyone with a semblance of intelligence would've known that. But it was, at that moment, the strongest stand I had ever taken against the boy who had hijacked my life nine years before. I was done being his victim.

Rather than go to homeroom, I made my way to the counselor's office to get my schedule changed. I might've been writing my own narrative, but I wasn't stupid!

5

HANNAH

P erfidious *(adj.) disloyal, unfaithful, traitorous, treasonous, two-faced*

I WAS MORE than happy to get out of math after seventy minutes of sneers from the Madisons, especially when I found out Katelyn was in my second period history class. Having someone —anyone—to navigate the halls of high school with was imperative.

The euphoria ended outside second period when I noticed that Madison T and Madysen H were headed in the same direction, shouldering others out of their way as they unleashed savage comments about people's clothes and hairstyles.

"They're in this class, too?" I whispered to Katelyn.

"Yep, and here comes Maddison Eagle—part three of the triumvirate." Katelyn pointed to a tall Black girl with dark, silky-smooth hair that melted over her shoulders in soft waves. My stomach dropped into the recesses of my shoes.

I took out my phone to check my own hair, which I had spent hours crafting into cascading, frizz-free locks that anyone who didn't know me would think came naturally.

Bruh! My mane was coming unraveled.

"I'm fairly sure the Madisons sit down as a unit with the counselor to register for classes. They've been in almost every class together since sixth grade. In eighth grade, a new counselor tried to separate them, and that didn't end well."

"Are you saying that if I have one in my class, I get them all?" I asked.

"Usually, but Maddison E is a year ahead in math. She took Math 2 in, like, second grade," Katelyn said. "Madison T—the figurehead of the group—really doesn't belong in the same classes as Maddison E or Madysen H. But if your parents cause a big enough stink, you can get whatever you want!"

We filed through the doorway behind the Madisons, who, I swear, whispered my name. In any other scenario, having the popular girls reciting my name two hours into the first day of school would be cause for celebration. This time—not so much. I was assured of this when I heard them follow my name with the phrase *forensic freak*.

I glanced around the room for two empty seats beside each other. Katelyn was quickly becoming my new best friend.

"Hannah—over here!" I heard Hank's voice before I saw his very conspicuous wave from the back of the room.

The *whole room* saw the wave and his spastic blinking.

"Oh look, *New Girl*," Madison T called over her shoulder in an unnecessarily loud voice. "There's your freak show BFF waving like one of those kids on the short bus."

Behind Madison T, Madysen H and Maddison E stole a look at each other. It was an almost undetectable show of humanity.

Hank heard her and immediately put his hand under the desk.

Katelyn tugged on my sleeve and whispered, "Ignore them. Trust me."

"Let's sit back there." Katelyn pointed to two vacant desks beside Hank.

"Um...." I hesitated and watched as the Madisons ordered people out of their seats so they could sit together.

Madison T said, "Save a place for Lexi and Jenna, too."

"Lexi got moved to regular history," Madysen H said. "She failed her state exam, so the counselor moved her out of honors."

Madison T clicked her tongue. "Like that matters. She just needs to have her mom call the counselor."

"Her parents don't let her get away with failing anything."

As they exchanged their best ideas on how to manipulate the system, I slipped in front of Katelyn so I wouldn't be stuck sitting next to Hank.

6

HANK

S chizophrenia is a disorder that affects how a person thinks, feels, and behaves. This mental illness is marked by thoughts or experiences that seem out of touch with reality, disorganized speech, and withdrawal from daily activities. There is no cure for schizophrenia, but treatments include medicine, psychotherapy, and behavioral therapy. See Forensics 411 *episode 42, "Dangerous Minds."*

IN SECOND PERIOD, Hannah stepped in front of Katelyn and parked herself in the vacant desk that wasn't next to mine.

I leaned past Katelyn to ask Hannah about her earlier class. She didn't even acknowledge me.

"Hey, *Hank*," Katelyn said. "You know, I totally forgot your name was actually Henry rather than Boomer."

I nodded and then, as an afterthought, added a smile. Dr. Blanchard said smiling at a person made them feel "heard" and "valued."

Hannah was focused straight forward on the teacher as if taking attendance was the most interesting thing she'd ever witnessed.

I tried again. "How was first period?"

No eye contact, but she did hold up her hand to let me know she couldn't take her attention from the teacher. I deduced that she was watching the attendance proceedings to learn the kids' names. It was a good move, so I tuned in, too.

"Henry Boyd?"

"Here." I raised my hand. "But I go by Hank."

Faces, both familiar and not, turned to me, and I heard the word "Boomer" whispered along with phrases like "recognize him... hair... different... on the news."

I listened with pride until Madison Talbot loudly and publicly said, "Freak show!"

"Psst," I tried to distract Hannah's attention from Madison T.

Her head snapped around. "What are you doing here?" she hissed. "When you showed me your schedule on the bus, we didn't have any classes together!"

My heart pounded in my chest. My hands began to sweat. My left leg started to tremble, which morphed into a more pronounced bounce. I reached in my pocket for my bit of foam— the remains of my stress ball.

It wasn't there.

Part of me drifted away and witnessed the tall, dark, wavy-haired boy reach for his backpack. I floated from above the scene as the boy went pocket to pocket in search of what the other kids called his "squishy."

"Are you okay?" Katelyn whispered as I started to breathe heavily, unable to find the bit of foam I desperately needed to squeeze.

"I need to find it," I whispered to myself.

"What?" Katelyn mumbled. "What do you need?"

"Nothing," I answered as my breathing became loud and fast.

The two girls sitting in front of me, neither of which I knew, turned around.

"Are you okay?" one of them asked.

Finally, my fingers found the piece of foam at the very bottom of my backpack. I squeezed it as hard as I could; closed my mouth so I could breathe deeply—and less obviously—through my nose.

Katelyn raised her hand. "Um, Mr. Anderson, I think Hank is sick."

I closed my eyes and hung my head low, trying to slow my breathing and convince the bouncing of my leg, the shaking of my hands, and the sound of my pounding heart to stop. This was not how I wanted to start the new school year.

Katelyn was up and talking quietly to the teacher, then she came back to me, picked up my backpack with my hand still stuffed in it, clutching the bit of stress ball.

"Come on," Katelyn said gently. "I'll take you to the nurse."

Hannah jumped out of her seat.

"Wait, Katelyn, I'll get your stuff."

As Katelyn ushered me out, I heard someone murmur "freak" and another mumble "diarrhea."

Was it better for them to assume I was having a gastrointestinal emergency or that sometimes the stress of life was too much for me?

Either way, I had made my impression on Honors History, and it wasn't a good one.

In the hallway, away from everybody, Katelyn took my hand. She had a sincere expression of concern on her face. "Are you having a panic attack?"

I questioned her with my eyes.

"Your mom told my mom."

I slid down the lockers into a crouching position. *Was nothing sacred between moms?*

"Here, let me," Hannah said.

She kneeled in front of me. "Keep breathing and give me your arms."

I held out my left arm but kept my right one in my backpack where it clung to the small piece of foam Dr. Blanchard prescribed for me back in sixth grade.

"It's okay. I'm going to use your pressure points, and I need both arms," she said.

I brought my right hand out of my backpack but didn't let go of my morsel of foam.

Hannah examined my clenched fist. "Is that your comfort object?"

I nodded through deep breaths.

She knew about comfort objects?

Hannah held both of my arms and massaged just above the inside of my wrists with her thumbs.

"Keep breathing and close your eyes. I'm going to move to your union valley point. It's right here," Hannah said, placing her hand on a spot between my thumb and index finger. "Do you think you can release your grasp so I can properly massage that other hand?"

I nodded slightly and handed my bit of foam to Katelyn.

Hannah took both my hands in hers and applied firm pressure in circles. My sweating had stopped, and I felt myself coming out of the tunnel I'd fallen through.

My breathing slowed, and my eyes met Hannah's.

"It's okay," she said. "I get them, too… sometimes."

Then she turned to Katelyn. "You don't have to tell anyone that."

"No, of course not," Katelyn said.

"They started after Ben died," Hannah explained.

"Who's Ben?" Katelyn asked.

Remembering my promise to Hannah, I didn't answer.

Hannah hesitated, then said, "My little brother—he was killed by a drunk driver when I was in fifth grade."

"Oh, gosh. That's awful," Katelyn said.

Hannah removed her hands from mine. "Is it okay if I rub your ears? There's a pressure point at the top of them. It's good for anxiety and insomnia."

"I didn't realize you practiced traditional Chinese medicine," I said.

Hannah smirked. "I'm full of surprises."

"Yes, you are," I said.

The three of us settled in a small circle outside Mr. Anderson's classroom.

"So, you're speaking to me?" I asked.

"Yes. Fine. I'm speaking to you!" Hannah answered.

"When were you not speaking to him?" Katelyn asked.

"At the beginning of history," I said. "Who got to you?"

Hannah didn't answer.

"Or was it just another spontaneous dissolution of our friendship meant to keep me on my toes?" I asked. Recalling the first time we met I said, "Maybe you really are schizophrenic!"

Hannah stood up.

"Wait," Katelyn said. "What's going on?"

"I think Hannah found out I'm not the 'local celebrity' she thought I was. She's weighing her options."

7

HANNAH

D*evolve (v.) to degenerate or decline gradually*

HANK CALLED behind me in the hall, but I kept going all the way to the girl's bathroom.

I dropped onto the toilet and cried. I didn't bawl. That would've been too productive. That would allow me to release the emotions I was feeling inside, and it would be more accept-able (and quiet) than letting out the prolonged scream that was growing inside me.

At least among kids our age, Hank was the punchline to their jokes. I watched my dreams of popularity circle the drain.

"Social downward mobility," I whispered.

I let my tears devolve into a self-pitying moan projected into a fistful of brittle, brown paper towels. When I was out of tears, I texted my mom from the bathroom and asked her to pick me up after school. I couldn't bear the state-funded transportation on such a monumentally disastrous first day of high school.

Oblivious to my day of torture, Dad bounced through the back door earlier than usual that day. "Looks like someone had a great day!" Mom said.

"The boat's in!" He danced a little jig. "We finally have a boat!"

Josey ran to the kitchen window to look at the dock. "Can we take a ride?"

"It's not *here*, here," Dad said, tousling her brown curls. "It was delivered to Fripp's Marina today. She's going to be our ticket to family fun!"

In a moment of insanity, Dad reached out to tousle my hair too. I dove to the side, caught his hand mid-air, and said, "Seriously, Dad, don't touch the hair."

"Sorry, lost my mind there for a second." He moved on to my mom, around whom he wrapped his arms. A blow torch couldn't take the smile off his face. You had to admire his optimism. He somehow thought that getting the family on a boat with the wind blowing through our hair would wipe away all the bad things we'd been through.

Nothing good ever came of a mash-up between my hair and the wind.

Nothing.

"They have to install the electronics still; that'll take a week," Dad said.

"You got a good stereo, right?" I asked. Dad gave us each one request for a feature on the boat. I asked for a stereo. Josey wanted one of those tubes you ride on behind the boat, and mom asked for a good navigation system so we wouldn't get lost.

"But of course," Dad answered. "We will be cruising along the waterway jamming to—"

"Don't say it!" I raised my hand to stop him from naming some lame song from the nineties that he and Mom used to "jam" to. The words to "Whoomp! There It Is" danced in his eyes.

"John, I thought you ordered this boat special for us. Why didn't they put all the electronics on in Florida before they shipped it?"

"I did my research."

Dad always did his research.

"The most common thing to go bad on a boat is the electronics. If I get the electronics installed locally, I can get them repaired locally and it will be under warranty."

"Can we go see it? Please, please, please!" Josey whined.

"I wouldn't mind a peek," Mom said. "Now that the dock's done, we'll be able to use it all the time."

Dad questioned me with his eyes, as if waiting for me to beg like an eight-year-old.

"Isn't gonna happen," I said. "The day I beg to go out in public with you people is the day you know it's time to send me back to the looney bin."

Mom glared at me and whispered, "Not funny."

THE SALES OFFICE and convenience store at Fripp's Boatyard and Marina were located along the water. Boaters could buy snacks, drinks, bait, and marine supplies. Beside that were the dry stacks, a two-walled building the size of an airplane hangar with boats stacked on metal shelves four boats high and about a dozen wide.

"Wow! Look at that!" Josey said, pointing at a forklift that was lowering a bright lime green boat from the top row of the dry stacks. "Which one's ours?"

"None of those," Dad answered.

"Is it one of *those*?" Josey asked aiming toward the fenced-in field containing much larger boats.

Some were stored on trailers for their owners; others, blocked for repair by the marina mechanics. Many old, abandoned ones lay off kilter, waiting either to be bought and refurbished or left to slowly crumble. Hank called that part Fripp's Graveyard.

"Those boats either belong to other people, they're for sale, or they're abandoned," I told her.

Mom stole a glance to ask how I knew that.

"Hank and I went on a bike ride back here last summer. He knows all about boats."

"Ours is brand new—never been used," Dad said. "It's over this way."

He led us past the dry stacks to a salty man I knew to be Old Man Fripp, the owner.

"There she is!" Dad said, pointing to a yellow boat on a trailer in the gravel parking lot beside the dry stacks. "Isn't she a beauty?" Dad took out his cell phone. "You guys get in front of her, so I can take your picture and some video."

"How do you know it's a girl?" Josey asked.

"All boats are considered female," Dad said, still videoing.

"Mr. Fripp!" Dad called and waved frantically, reminding me of Hank in history class.

Mr. Fripp crossed the parking lot.

"I'm John Simmons. I ordered this yellow twenty-three-foot center console." He motioned with his head.

Mr. Fripp shook his hand. "Oh, right." Then he studied me for an uncomfortable second.

Did he remember me from the summer when he caught Hank and me wandering around the boat graveyard, allegedly looking for my dog?

"The boat just arrived today so we haven't installed the electronics yet. It'll be about a week."

"That's fine. We were just excited to see it," Dad said.

Old Man Fripp narrowed his gaze on me. "Don't I know you?"

I shook my head. "Um, no sir. I don't think so."

"You might have seen her in the paper or on the news," Dad

said. "She helped break the McFarland missing person case in July."

"She's quite the hero," Mom said, squeezing my shoulder.

"Took down half the police department, which ain't good for us business owners," Old Man Fripp said. "We depend on the cops around here, especially at night."

I could tell that irritated Dad.

"I believe there's an acting police chief right now and that the town council is searching for a new mayor. I'm sure it will all work out."

"Let's hope so," Fripp said. "I'd hate to see some kind of crime spree in Vista Point because two kids decided to play detective."

"It'll be ready in about a week?" Mom asked. "That's perfect timing because they just finished our dock."

"You got a lift?" Mr. Fripp asked.

"I was just going to tie her up to our dock," Dad said.

"You on a tidal creek?" Old Man Fripp asked.

"No, the Intracoastal Waterway."

Old Man Fripp shook his head in disapproval. "If you tie that boat up on the ICW, she's gonna get beat harder than a sissy in gym class. You should either install a boat lift, keep it on the trailer, or store it here in dry dock." He pointed to the open-air boat storage facility. "We just built this. If you store with us, all you do is call an hour ahead, and one of my boys will take your boat off the dry stacks and put her in the water. Then you hop on your boat over yonder at the docks. She won't get beat up in the ICW, and you don't have the expense and maintenance of having your own boat lift."

"I'd really like to have the boat right behind our house so we can just hop on anytime we want," Dad said.

"You're better off storing her in dry stack," Mr. Fripp said. "It's cheaper, safer, and more convenient than keeping it on a trailer."

"Do you have room for us in your stacks?" Dad asked.

Old Man Fripp's nodded slowly. "Sure do."

"What do you think, Jen?" Dad asked.

"Let's see how much a lift costs and how quickly we can get one built. If it comes down to it, we can always keep it on the trailer in the driveway," Mom said.

"When you keep your boat on a trailer, you need to drive to a boat ramp every time you want to launch it, then put it back on the trailer when you're done. Our boat ramp over there"—Old Man Fripp pointed past the marina convenience store—"is the only one nearby that's free. It stays busy in the summer, is a madhouse on the weekends, and people get mighty impatient with boaters that don't know what they're doing." He raised his eyebrows as if to accuse Dad of being an amateur who'd most definitely anger his fellow boaters.

"Well, thanks for that info. You've definitely given us some things to think about," Dad said.

"No worries. Just be sure you take all the costs into account and the amount of protection and convenience we can offer."

8

HANK
TUESDAY

Burglary involves a person illegally entering a property with intent to commit a crime. Even if nothing is stolen, the property has still been "burglarized." Robbery is when someone takes something of value directly from another person by force or intimidation. See Forensics 411 episode 12, "Crossing the Line," for more details.

THE FOLLOWING DAY, Hannah didn't ride the bus and successfully ignored my existence in second period.

At lunch, I got my tray of fat-breeding carbs, tepid milk, and fatigued vegetables and settled at one of the small tables along the wall unofficially reserved for the friendless.

I was focused on my so-called lunch when a French fry landed in my shriveled, gray peas.

I spotted Katelyn waving at me from across several tables.

Breathing a sigh of relief, I moved to sit with her. As soon as I settled in, Hannah was at the cash register with her lunch. Katelyn waved her over and added a third chair to the table.

I groaned.

For a nanosecond, Hannah and I scrutinized each other, then

buried our heads in the worst the US Department of Agriculture had to offer America's children.

"Okay, people," Katelyn said in a low voice, "talk."

Hannah turned on me. "What *is* your childhood trauma?"

My eyes met Katelyn's, then we both glanced away.

"Do you have Tourette's or something?" Hannah asked.

Katelyn squirmed.

"If you want someone without pre-existing conditions, I'm not that person."

"I've got asthma." Katelyn waved an inhaler at us.

"Tourette's isn't contagious or anything," I said. "I just have involuntary movements. They started in kindergarten. They're worse when I'm stressed." I leaned back and crossed my arms. "Sorry if you were expecting a full medical disclosure from me."

"Are you stressed right now?" Hannah asked.

"Gee, I don't know. You're my friend; you're not my friend. You're helping me, then you're running away. Forgive me if I'm a little nauseated as you hurtle through Plutchik's Wheel of Emotions."

"Plutchik's Wheel of Emotions?" Hannah said.

Mild-mannered, borderline-shy Katelyn threw her hands in the air and groused at us. "This is not how this is supposed to go! I brought you two here so you can make up—be friends—get along. Quit arguing!"

Hannah glanced around the cafeteria.

Katelyn lowered her voice and leaned into the middle of the table. "You two are ruining my plan."

"Plan?" Hannah and I said at the same time.

"Have you noticed that Ashton moved away?"

"Who's Ashton?" Hannah asked.

"My best friend since third grade. Her dad got transferred to Japan." Katelyn's voice cracked. She gazed over at the table of Madisons who were pointing at a large girl in a small skirt and snickering in the most obvious and cruel way. "I thought we could form a group... for protection in the Madisons' war against human kindness. There's safety in numbers."

"Sorry," Hannah mumbled into the stale bun that enveloped a meat-like product.

"Sorry for *now*," I said. "but how will you be feeling in another ten minutes, Bipolarina."

"Ooh, burn!" Hannah gibed.

"Seriously!" Katelyn smacked her hand on the table. "Stop bickering!"

"I'll stop if she can keep her multiple personalities in check."

Katelyn waved a finger at me. "That's just the kind of thing I'm talking about."

Hannah and I grumbled.

"Have you heard about the robbery at the marina?"

I sat up straight. "What?"

"*Fripp's* Marina?" Hannah asked.

"Yeah, my dad's a mechanic there," Katelyn said.

"I was just there yesterday after school!"

"You were?" I asked.

"The boat my dad ordered came in yesterday."

I leaned toward Katelyn. "What did your dad tell you?"

"Not much. He said it looks like the robbers got away with a lot of valuable stuff."

"Boats?" I asked.

"He didn't say."

"The police department is stretched pretty thin right now," I said. "Corker, Marcia Masters, that JoAnne Lubbock, and another deputy are all that's left since we busted Chief Buckley."

"I heard your mom's dating Officer Corker," Katelyn said with a coy smile.

"Really?" Hannah said. "Your mom and Steve? That's awesome!"

I didn't think it was *awesome*. "Hopefully, it won't last any longer than when she took up roller-blading."

"Women have needs, you know," Hannah said. "They can't just—"

"Don't even finish that sentence!" I said, threatening her with my finger. "Katelyn, can we talk to your dad? I'd like to get as much information as we can before the trail goes cold."

Katelyn smiled. "I was hoping you'd want to investigate. I can help, right?"

"Of course," I said, then turned to Hannah. "You are currently on probation. If you prove yourself unable to keep your inner Sybils in line, you're done."

"What's an *innersibles*?" Katelyn asked.

"Probably some serial killer from yesteryear," Hannah said with a roll of her eyes.

"Sybil," I said. "Haven't you ever seen the movie or read the book? Or, for Pete's sake, seen *Forensics 411* episode 42? Sybil was the alias for Shirley Mason, a woman who had sixteen separate personalities. At the time, no one was known to have that many. They had different names, ages, and genders. They even had unique voices and mannerisms. Back then, in the 1950s, they called it multiple personalities or split personalities. Today it's called Dissociative Identity Disorder—often abbreviated as D-I-D. It's a mental illness where people shut off or dissociate themself from a situation that's too traumatic to process in their conscious mind. They take on another personality who doesn't have to deal with that trauma. The other identities might not know about each other, and they can even do things that the other identities don't remember. You need to watch episode 42."

"FYI, Katelyn," Hannah said, "sometimes he gives homework."

"Trust me," Katelyn said. "I've known that one"—she pointed to me—"since before he was even called Boomer. I remember back in the day when he was just little old Henry Boyd."

"Sounds like *I'm* not the one with multiple personalities, Henry-Boomer-Hank!" Hannah said.

I narrowed my glare at her. "A name change over time is *not* the same thing as DID. You seriously need to watch episode 42. I get into the case of Billy Milligan, who was one of the first Americans to use the multiple personality defense in criminal proceedings. It turned out, he may have had up to twenty-four personalities and one of them—not Billy—committed several rapes. He was declared NGRI and put in a mental institution."

"NGRI?" Hannah asked.

"Not guilty by reason of insanity," I said. "Your dad's an attorney. You should know the terminology."

"He does like, I don't know, contracts or something. It's not like we sit around the dinner table discussing acronyms for legal terms."

"Okay, stop right there!" Katelyn said. "This is about to turn into another argument, and I will not tolerate more bickering."

"Sorry, *Mom!*" Hannah said.

Katelyn shrank a bit into her seat.

"Let's meet at my house after school," I said. "Four-thirty. Bring your bike and we'll take a ride over to Fripp's." I turned to Hannah. "Should I expect Dr. Jekyll or Mrs. Hyde to show up in fourth period?"

She curled her lip. "I'll surprise you!"

Katelyn threw her hands in the air and said, "Okay, I give up!"

AFTER SCHOOL, I settled at the end of our dock and listened. With little wind, it was so quiet that sounds carried over the water forever. I watched a boat out in the saltmarsh putter along and stop intermittently to check crab pots.

The dock vibrated as Chaucer ran toward me. I turned to watch him gallop in my direction, but he wasn't alone. Hannah was with him.

Chaucer skidded to a stop and let out a joyful howl.

Hannah removed her shoes and socks and took a seat beside me. Chaucer nuzzled her ear and thumped his tail.

"Hey, boy!" She wrapped her arms around his neck then stroked his ears. "I've missed you!"

I scoffed. "You're early."

"I needed the unconditional love of a good dog."

"Do me a favor and don't give him whiplash with your mood changes. We can't afford any more big vet bills."

Hannah nodded. "Okay, I deserved that. I admit it. I've been a bit volatile lately."

Chaucer lay down and put his head in her lap, staring up at her with droopy, adoring brown eyes.

"Ya think?"

She shifted her weight on the dock and stroked Chaucer's fur.

"I know my mom told you about how I kind of lost it after Ben died."

I nodded. "I promised you I wouldn't tell anybody about Ben, and I haven't."

Hannah dipped her feet in the water and cleared her throat. "So, as you figured out, Ben was hit by a car in front of our elementary school. That... horrible, horrible crone ran up on the curb and hit him and two of his friends. Ben took the brunt of it. She was drunk at three o'clock in the afternoon. I should've been there. I'd been talking to some friends about a sleep-over and was late meeting him. Mom was a few cars back in the carpool line and saw the whole thing."

Hannah sniffled.

"By the time I made it to the front of the school, it had already happened. Ben was still alive when we got to the hospital. They took him to surgery because they could tell by the purple marks on his stomach and chest that he had internal bleeding." Hannah's voice choked up. "He didn't make it."

"That's awful," I mumbled.

"Have you ever lost someone you loved?" she asked.

"My grandma died of cancer when I was in third grade."

"Is that why you live with your grandfather?"

"No, we've lived here since before I was born. I think it's because it was cheaper for my mom as a single parent. And since Grandpa started getting dementia, he needs our help."

Hannah nodded.

"I'm sorry I've been... difficult. It's just... it's been hard... ever since Ben died—and it's been almost four years now. Mom told you about how I had to go into the hospital." She splashed her feet around in the water. "It wasn't a *regular* hospital. I wasn't there to have my tonsils taken out, *if you know what I mean*. And well, your jokes about mental health aren't that funny to me."

Her words shrank me to a microscopic version of myself.

"Oh, wow... I..." I buried my head in my hands. I should've known better. I summoned all my strength, made the most direct eye contact I'd ever made, and said, "I'm really sorry. That was stupid."

"It's okay," she said. "I know I'm not the easiest person to understand. I get that I've been kind of volatile. I just wanted to be popular here, instead of floating between crazy girl and invisible wallflower like I did in middle school. I had friends in elementary school. But after I got out of the hospital, I felt like all people did was whisper about me."

"I take it you found out you can't be popular if you're friends with *me*," I said. "That didn't take long. The Madisons must really be working on their messaging to have gotten to you on the first day of school."

"No, it's not..." she said. "You said you were a local celebrity."

"*I* never said that. *You* said that! If you were thinking you could rise to popularity on my coat tails, that's not gonna happen."

I stood up.

She grabbed my hand. "Wait, don't leave." She pulled me back down but didn't release my hand.

"It's hard because we *are* friends and I like you—weird as you are." She smiled. "And you talk to me." Her voice cracked. "I had forgotten what it was like to have fun… to laugh… to trust someone."

"And I screwed that up, I get it. I let my need for information override my… well, I don't know what it overrode, but I get that I was wrong. And just so you know, it was all me. Dr. Blanchard never told me anything about you."

She nodded and released my hand. "I figured that out later, after I thought things through. Look, I *thought* I wanted to be popular, but I don't. I want to be your friend instead."

"Is that supposed to be a compliment?"

She stared out at the water. "Don't you realize that people make fun of you?"

"You think it's something new? That it *just started*?" I rolled my eyes.

"Hank, they talk about you all the time! I've heard them. They make fun of your web show and how you blink all the time, and your…"

"*Do they*? Well, you better call the cops and alert the press! Some cretins think I'm not good enough for them! Well, you know what"—I took a deep breath and slowed down—"maybe they're right. I *don't* live in a fancy house or have expensive clothes. I don't have a dad who's a lawyer, or a mom who can afford to not work. We have one car that my mom drives to work, and it's used. She saves every cent she can, so I can go to college. I have better things to do than go to The Compound and get wasted. The Madisons, Dillon, and all those morons are going to peak in high school. They will never know that they can want more than *this* out of life." I motioned to our surroundings. "If they weren't such jerks, I'd feel bad for them," I said. "Besides, I'd rather be disliked for what I am, than admired for what I'm not."

Tears crept down her cheeks. "I wanted you to be popular." She sniffled.

"Well, I'm not."

She wiped her running nose.

"Hannah, even though nearly everyone feels like it's their personal mission to make me understand that I'm wildly different from them, it's taken a long time to realize that that's not a bad thing. Yeah, I have tics, unique interests, and some other idiosyncrasies. I'm smarter than most of my teachers, and I've come to understand that it's better that I *not* point that out to them. It took every bit of courage I'd ever had to wave to you that day we met."

"Aww," she said, "That's sweet, and I'm a jerk. I want to be more like you."

"It gets lonely," I said.

"But it doesn't have to be," she said. "If we stick together… you, me… Katelyn."

"You're the one who seems to be the variable in that equation."

"Well, I'm going to stop that," she said. "I'm going to be a constant."

"Really?" I said. "You keep saying that, but then you spin off in the other direction." I swallowed hard and said something that I never could've imagined myself saying three months earlier. "I deserve better than that."

"I mean it this time," she said. "And I really am sorry for all I have done since the police station. I've been conflicted."

At that moment Katelyn came up behind us. "Hey you two. Are you being nice?"

We both nodded convincingly enough that she ignored Hannah's tears.

9

HANNAH

F *raternal (adj.) siblings from the same pregnancy that result when two separate ova are fertilized. Each twin is genetically distinct so they can be different sexes and have different appearances. See also dizygotic*

I COULDN'T WAIT to get my license and not have to schlep around town on a bicycle. But on that day, Hank, Katelyn, and I schlepped.

"Last night when we went to see our new boat, Old Man Fripp really stared me down. I think he remembered me from the summer."

"We might need to dust off your run-away dog story," Hank said. "That way he'll remember why you look familiar—you're constantly searching for your badly behaved dog."

"Why's *my* imaginary dog gotta have behavior issues? Why can't we be hunting for Chaucer?"

"Because Chaucer is disciplined, and borderline perfect."

"I seem to remember trudging across Pelican Island searching for your *disciplined* dog."

"He was on a case. We just didn't know it. Plus, his hyperactive olfactory system allowed us to solve Vista Point's crime of the century, thereby putting you, Miss-Newcomer-To-Town-That-Nobody-Would-Otherwise-Know, on the map."

I rolled my eyes. "Yeah, that's been great for me. I'm Forensic Freak's BFF!"

"Actually, Dillon Buckley calls you 'Fro White.'"

"I thought I had successfully negotiated a ceasefire between you two," Katelyn said.

We rode directly to the repair shop at Fripp's boatyard as if we belonged, and no one seemed to notice. Crime tape stretched the length of the bottom row of boats on the dry stacks. The fork-lift was at the end of the stacks nearest the water, lowering a boat from the second row.

"Hmm," I said, looking around. "I don't see our boat. It was over there last night." I pointed.

"Maybe Daddy's working on it in the shop," Katelyn said.

KATELYN'S DAD, Phil Calhoun, wore dark blue coveralls and latex gloves covered in black grease.

"Hi, Daddy," Katelyn said. "These are my friends, Hannah Simmons and Hank—you remember Hank, don't you?"

"Boomer?" Mr. Calhoun said studying him. "Man, you've grown! I haven't seen you in forever."

"He goes by *Hank* now," I said.

Why did I feel the need to keep telling everyone that?

"Mr. Phil," Hank said as he scanned the shop, "we wanted to talk to you about the robbery."

Turning to Katelyn, her dad said, "Are we going to see your picture in the paper next?"

Hank held his phone up and shot video of Mr. Calhoun's workplace. He didn't even look at the screen.

"You know the police department is small to begin with," Hank said, "and since we exposed Chief and Mayor Buckley's wrong-doings, the department is down to a skeleton crew. Officer Corker's the acting chief until they hold a special election in November. He asked for our help. What can you tell us about the robbery?"

He aimed his camera at Mr. Calhoun.

"They cut the lock off the fence to get into the boatyard. That center bay door of my shop was open when I got here this morning. The thieves must've used my engine hoist to remove engines from the bottom row of boats on the stacks. The hoist was next to the stacks this morning." He pointed in that direction.

"We store the boats that are too heavy for the forklift over in the fenced grassy area. The heavier boats under twenty-eight feet —usually ones with two or more engines—are stored on the lowest row. An engine can weigh more than five-hundred pounds. When we store the boats, the heaviest go on the bottom, the lightest are always higher up."

Mr. Calhoun moved toward the open bay door.

"The thieves took one boat on a trailer. I hadn't installed the electronics yet. They used Emmitt's truck to get the boat to the ramp."

"Emmitt?" Hank asked.

"That's Grady Fripp's son. It's a family business. Both his boys, Emmitt and Brock, work here. They're twins. Two peas in a pod—always have been," Mr. Calhoun said. "They're almost thirty, and still do everything together. They even live together. If they're lucky, they'll find a set of female twins to marry, and they can all live happily ever after."

"Did they just hit the boats on the stacks, or did they steal from the larger ones over in the field?" Hank asked.

"They got all the boats on the bottom row of the dry stacks for sure, but Emmitt and Brock are lowering every boat from the higher levels to check for a gaping hole where the electronics should be. Obviously, you can tell from ground level if any of the higher boats are missing an engine," Mr. Calhoun said. "If you ask me, it's a waste of time. Our burglar would have to be Spider-Man to climb the dry stacks, especially with an armful of electronics. One of the cops went through the trailered boats in the yard, and it didn't appear anything was missing. A lot of those boats have in-board motors that would be too hard to steal. But Grady's calling all the owners, too, just to let them know about the burglary."

"You said they took a boat on a trailer," I said. "Our new boat was just delivered here yesterday…"

"Was it a yellow center-console Sea Runner?"

"It was yellow. I didn't pay attention to the brand. It was on a trailer over there." I pointed near the dry stacks.

"Sorry." Mr. Calhoun shook his head. "I think the thieves got your boat."

"My dad is going to be seriously mad."

"If it's any consolation, they left the trailer," Mr. Calhoun said.

"And you say the burglars used Emmitt's truck to tow the Sea Runner to the boat ramp? How do you know?" Hank said.

"They just left it there. Boat trailer was at the ramp, hooked to the truck." Mr. Calhoun turned to me. "At least one of the thieves left here by water."

"Are there security cameras?" Hank asked. "Did they catch any images of the thieves?"

"I haven't seen any of the footage yet, but from what Grady says, the only security camera working was the one in my shop."

"They were all broken?" Katelyn asked.

"Dead batteries," her dad answered.

"All of them?" I asked.

"Yep. I keep the camera in the shop charged, but one of the boys does the other cameras. I guess they fumbled that one."

"Does the shop camera have a tape in it?"

"No, it's all digital and the video feed goes to Fripp's office computer."

Mr. Calhoun pointed to two boats inside the shop.

Hank aimed his phone at them, took some still shots, then went back to recording.

"I was putting a top-of-the-line navigation system in that cuddy cabin over there, and the thieves took the whole thing. That center console was getting a multifunction display system with GPS, VHF radio, satellite radio, chart plotter, and a fish finder worth eleven thousand dollars. They took a lot of the boxed equipment I had on my shelves, too."

Hank stared out the open bay of the shop. "Where are the other cameras located?"

"One at the entrance to the store, one inside the store, one at the entrance gate and two at the wet slips. Fripp hadn't installed any cameras on the stacks yet."

Mr. Calhoun tipped his head toward the side wall. "I've spent today going through my purchase orders and matching them up with what boxed equipment is still in the shop to figure out exactly what they took."

Katelyn's dad led us outside to a safe distance from the fork-lift. Hank continued videoing and taking photos with his phone.

"That's Emmitt with the blond hair; Brock has brown. They're fraternal twins."

Emmitt was in the forklift dabbing the sweat from his fore-head with a handkerchief.

"Can we ask them some questions?" Hank said.

"The cops questioned them this morning."

"I'd still like to ask them a couple things."

Mr. Calhoun introduced us to Emmitt. Brock had gone into the store.

"Y'all are just kids," Emmitt said. "What's your interest in this case?"

"My parents' brand-new boat was stolen," I said.

"We heard the thieves used your truck to move her boat from the gravel over to the ramp," Hank said. "Is that right?"

Emmitt curled his lip. "Damn thing wouldn't start at the end of the day yesterday, so I had to leave it here overnight. Those crooks must've got it started and used it to steal the boat!" He shook his head in disbelief. "I wonder if one of 'em was a mechanic or something." He glanced toward the shop.

"What was wrong with your truck?" Hank said.

"Just wouldn't start."

"Did you try jump-starting it?" Hank asked.

"Yeah."

"Did your brother help you with that?"

"With what?"

"With jump-starting your truck," Hank said.

"It doesn't take two people to jump start a truck." Emmitt sounded irritated.

"And you checked the cable connections?"

"Of course!" Emmitt said. "I'm not an idiot!"

"How'd you get home yesterday?" I asked.

"Brock."

Emmitt's cell phone rang. He fished a smart phone out of his pocket, examined the screen, put it back, and took a flip phone from his other back pocket.

"Look, Sherlock, I gotta take this call. You kids need to stand clear of the forklift."

We headed back to the shop.

"Do they live around here?" Hank asked Mr. Calhoun.

"They rent a house over on Gravely Street."

That was where Officer Corker lived.

"Are the marina and boatyard insured?" Hank asked.

"We have property insurance, and that covers theft, damage, or someone getting injured here. But Fripp's insurance doesn't cover the boats that people store here, the ones that are in for repair, or ones that were ordered directly from the manufacturer and delivered here. It's up to the individual owners to insure their boats. If something was stolen from your boat and you don't have insurance, you're out of luck."

"Could the boat owners lie about what kind of electronics they had?" Hank asked. "Say they had a more expensive brand of GPS than they actually had—or does Old Man Fripp have a record of exactly what equipment was on each boat?"

"I doubt Fripp has a record of that stuff. He's not exactly detail oriented. *If* Fripp were replacing the stolen stuff, I can see how it would be tempting for the boat owners to say they had top-of-the-line brand A electronics rather than cheap brand B. However, Fripp hasn't offered to do that—and I doubt he will. It would buy him some goodwill, but it would cost him hundreds of thousands of dollars. He doesn't have that kind of money, especially after just building the dry stacks."

"*That* much was stolen?" I asked.

"We don't have a firm number yet. I wouldn't be surprised if, when we've documented everything that was stolen, the thieves got close to a million dollar's-worth of stuff."

"Hannah," Katelyn said, "maybe Mr. Fripp's insurance will cover your boat since your dad got it here."

Mr. Calhoun shook his head. "Her boat came from Florida and was delivered here so I could install the electronics. Fripp's insurance only covers *his* inventory." He pointed to the wall of boxes. "They got your electronics, too."

"I did some research today," Hank said. "In July, marinas in Hilton Head and Charleston were robbed. In August, one in Myrtle Beach was hit. Similar scenario, but only electronics were taken. The IAMA—that's the International Association of Marine Investigators—says Kamaha motors over 200 horsepower, and equipment made by Grumin are popular targets. Apparently, professional thieves don't like Scanasonic brand equipment, even though it's top quality."

Mr. Calhoun chuckled. "These thieves know their stuff. Scanasonic integrates an anti-theft tracking device into their electronics. They haven't had success with a device that can be tracked *anywhere* in the world, but they're getting closer."

"I read about that," Hank said. "Scanasonic uses internet tracking technology that, obviously, can only work in places with internet service."

"Hannah, boats on trailers are easy targets," Mr. Calhoun said, "plus, your boat had two three-hundred-horse-power Kamaha engines."

Mr. Calhoun bent down to wipe a drop of oil off the shop floor. "A lot of marine thieves in the US have connections in the Caribbean. They steal the engines and electronics, transport them to a port, where the goods are taken over to the Caribbean on cargo carriers."

"Daddy?" Katelyn said. "How could the thieves steal so many engines so fast? I've watched you do it before, and it takes you a good bit to remove an engine."

"The complicated part is properly detaching all the cables. These thieves just cut the cables, disconnected the engine from the boat with a bolt extractor, then used my engine hoist to move them off the boat. They must've used a heavy-duty truck for their getaway."

"Do the people that buy the stolen stuff know it's stolen?"

"Usually. The thieves sell to retailers in the Caribbean, not individuals," Hank said.

"The businesses that buy the stolen goods from the theft ring know to keep their mouths shut or they'll get cut out of the scheme," Mr. Calhoun added.

"Do you think Old Man Fripp will talk to us?" Hank asked.

"Not today. He is in an unbelievably bad mood," Mr. Calhoun said. "Are you *sure* the cops asked for your help?"

"The acting chief of police is Hank's mom's *boyfriend*!" I said, knowing it drove him crazy when I used the B word.

Hank glared at me.

"Chief Corker is slammed. He asked me to do some leg work for him," Hank said with a confidence that made me wonder if Steve really *had* asked for his help.

"Daddy, I'm gonna ride home with Hank and Hannah."

"Okay, Sugar-Pie. Be careful," Mr. Calhoun said.

10

HANK

E ach year Gordon Thomas Honeywell Governmental Affairs *(GTH-GA), an international authority on DNA databases, selects a "DNA Hit of the Year." Law enforcement agencies from across the globe submit case files where DNA played an important role in solving the case. The award is meant to highlight the significance DNA databases play in identifying missing persons, solving crimes, and exonerating the innocent. See* Forensics 411 *episode 35, "All About That Base," to learn more.*

WHEN I GOT home from the boatyard, Corker's patrol car was in our driveway, but Mom's car wasn't.

"This can't be good," I mumbled to myself.

Corker was sitting at our kitchen table with his hand in a package of chocolate chip cookies. Grandpa was pouring milk.

"What's going on?"

"Found Henry walking down Walnut Street. "

"Grandpa! You're not supposed to go anywhere when we're gone!"

"You go to school. Angela goes to work, and I'm stuck here

all day waiting to see the next big thing that happens in Port Charles." He pointed in the direction of the den.

"What?" *Was Grandpa's dementia getting so bad he thought we lived somewhere else?*

"Port Charles is the setting of *General Hospital*," Corker explained. "My mom's a big fan."

"Grandpa, while I would be more than happy to let you take my place at school, I can't. And you know you have dementia. What if you left the house and couldn't remember how to get back home?"

"I'm not that bad off. I knew where I was going, and I knew how to get back. I've lived in this town my entire life!"

"He had a bag full of stuff from the dollar store," Corker said.

"Everything there costs *one* dollar!" Grandpa said. "Do you know how much you can get for ten bucks at that place?"

"Ten items?" I said.

"Nah, only nine 'cause of sales tax." Grandpa winked. "That was a trick question, and you failed!"

I shook my head. "You can't leave the house alone. That's all there is to it."

"It's my damn house, and I'm not a child!"

He grabbed the bag of cookies and his glass of milk and stormed out of the kitchen.

"You might want to get him one of those GPS tracking bracelets," Steve said. "It's kind of like what we use when a person is under house arrest."

"I'll talk to Mom about it," I said. "Um... thanks for bringing him home."

Corker patted me on the shoulder. "You're welcome, Buddy."

Jeez! He thinks we're friends now?

"So, what's up with the robbery at Fripp's?" I asked.

"You heard about that?"

"My friend Katelyn told me. Her dad, Phil Calhoun, is the head mechanic. His security camera was the only one working the night of the robbery. Did you see anything important on the camera footage?"

"The thieves wore masks and gloves so you can't see anything."

Mom came in the back door looking flustered and set her brief case on the counter. "Is everything okay?"

"I found your dad walking along Walnut Street an hour ago."

Mom let out a sigh. "Really?"

"I was telling Hank about a GPS bracelet you can get for him so you can keep track of where he is."

Mom nodded. "Yeah, we might need to do that."

"Fripp's Boatyard and Marina got robbed," I said.

"That's too bad," Mom said.

"The thieves stole Hannah's family's new boat."

"Really?" Corker said. "I knew they took one boat but didn't know it was theirs. That's too bad. Fripp said that boat was worth almost two hundred thousand dollars."

"I'm happy to take a peek at the security camera footage. A fresh set of eyes may spot something you didn't."

"Boom—*Hank*," Mom said. "I'm going to get used to calling you 'Hank,' I swear! You don't need to get involved in another police investigation. Last summer was bad enough, with that crazy Rodney Buckley attacking you and Hannah."

"Mom, it's a *robbery*. I'm nearly positive it was conducted by professional thieves who are long gone from here. That's how they work."

"You don't think it was locals?" Steve said.

"Do *you*?"

"Honestly, I haven't had much time to think about it. There's been a rash of shoplifting downtown. Rodney Buckley set fire to that school bus he lives in and now we can't find him."

"Someone let that mute maniac out on bail?" Mom said.

"All the Buckleys posted bail for themselves. It's not like they're murderers. They just have to stay inside county lines,"

Corker said. "I'm also investigating two bulls that went missing from a farm in Appleton, and we've got somebody skimming credit card numbers from a gas pump over on the northside of town. I only have three deputies in the entire department. Marcia is holding down the fort at the station. JoAnna Lubbock's patrolling the west side of the county, which leaves me and Jerry Cantrell on the east side where most of the population, the boat-yard, and the shoplifters are. Jerry's got a three-month-old and his wife's been on him to be home more."

"Have you questioned the people that live near the boat-yard?" I asked.

"I hope to get to that by the end of the week."

"I could do it for you, just to help you out."

Mom was rummaging through the pots and pans. "How many times do I have to say it? I don't want you involved in any more crime investigations!"

"Questioning the neighbors about what they saw isn't dangerous. Seriously. Hannah and I can do it together. We'll just knock on some doors, ask if they saw or heard anything, then move on to the next house. It's no more dangerous than selling Girl Scout cookies."

Corker ran one hand through his hair. "I *could* use some help."

"I don't like it," Mom said as she rather aggressively placed a pan on the stove.

Corker went to the stove, put his arms on her shoulders and whispered in her ear.

I didn't catch it all, but I did hear, "… need… accept… part of your life."

I went to the cabinet for a glass.

He sat back down and said, "You two did do a great job with the McFarland case."

"*And* we were the ones that figured out you were missing after Rodney kidnapped you."

"True."

"Then it's settled. Hannah and I will interview the neighbors near the boatyard. We'll take notes on everything for you."

"I don't know..." Mom said. "I know you live for this stuff, and it was fine when you were just making videos, but you're not a police officer. You're fourteen."

"I'll be fifteen in a couple of weeks."

I explained to Steve about the marina thefts in South Carolina over the summer and that the burglars might be moving northward.

"Trust me, the thieves are no longer in Vista Point," I said with confidence. "Fripp's was just another job for them. They were in and out, and now they've moved on." I whispered to Steve, "Can you email the shop security video to me?"

"No!" Mom spun around and glared at Steve. "You can't!"

"Mom, I'll watch it here at home. Watching a video *is not dangerous.*"

Corker let out a huge yawn. "You can't show it to anyone."

"Not even Hannah?"

He purposely avoided eye contact with Mom.

"*Just* Hannah," Corker said. "I don't want Grady Fripp to get wind that I've got kids helping with his case."

"They are *not* helping with the case," Mom insisted.

"Mom," I said, "I'm selling cookies and watching videos —that's it."

"I give up!" Mom threw her hands in the air.

"Do you know exactly what was stolen off each boat yet?" I asked.

"Nope. I'm not sure if Grady has even notified all the owners yet," Corker said. "I want to put a BOLO out to all the pawn shops once I get a list of what was stolen. Marcia is sending out a notice to all the marinas on the east coast to watch for the Simmons's boat."

He could issue as many be-on-the-lookout notices as he wanted. It wasn't going to help locate the stolen goods.

"I really don't think these thieves are going to be pawning

what they stole, and especially not locally. They're profession-als." I lowered my voice. "When can you send me the video?"

"My laptop's out in my patrol car. I'll email it to you later."

"Steve, do you think that's a good idea?" Mom asked.

"He's just going to study some photos on his computer. That's not dangerous," he said. "Hank has a good eye."

"Steve." (I called him by his first name when I wanted him to think I liked him.) "Did you collect any DNA and fingerprint evidence from the crime scene?"

"We dusted for fingerprints, but after Cantrell watched the shop security video and saw that the thieves wore gloves and masks, I didn't bother to send them off to the crime lab. There's no way they left any fingerprints behind with gloves on."

"What about trace evidence like clothing fibers? Maybe someone scratched themselves and left some blood. Did you do a luminol test?" I asked. "How about shoe prints or tire tracks?"

Corker scratched his stomach. "It's a robbery, not a murder."

"DNA evidence has been used to solve plenty of robberies. In fact, this year's *DNA Hit of the Year* was a robbery."

"I don't have the resources or time to search for DNA evidence in a property crime. Do you have any idea how much it costs to process one DNA sample?"

"About a thousand dollars."

"Exactly!" Corker said. "The department doesn't have that kind of money."

"The SBI does. Why don't you call Agent Watts and see if he can send some state CSI investigators down from Raleigh to do it for you. A lot of property crimes are committed by repeat offend-ers. It's possible our thieves' DNA is out there in a database just waiting to be matched to DNA they left behind in the shop or on one of the boats. Didn't you read the article about DNA and property crimes in last month's journal from the National Insti-tute of Justice? We could get a cold hit!"

Steve put his hand on my shoulder and said, "I had to let my subscription lapse because of budget cuts."

"Luckily," I said, "Hannah and I work for free."

11

HANNAH

D*espondent (adj.) in low spirits because of loss of hope or courage*

AFTER AN EXHAUSTING DAY playing both private investigator and high school whack-a-mole, I went home and crashed on my bed.

Face up.

Staring at the ceiling.

Wishing.

I reached between my bed and the wall and retrieved the wooden picture frame. I focused on the picture of Ben, Josey, and me. We looked as if we'd never had as much fun as that day at Disney World. I touched Ben's curly hair in the photo, wishing I could tousle it and call him *Goofus* like I used to.

I shut my eyes and tried to hear his voice. It was getting harder and harder to remember what he sounded like. If he were still alive, he'd be twelve and a half. Would his voice be changing yet? Would he be sprouting up taller than me? or would he still be the little thing he'd been at nine when Helen Tate ran him down, shattering my family forever?

I thought back to fifth grade and the weeks after Ben died. Revisiting those memories still hurt.

MOM TAPPED on my closed door with her knuckle and shrieked at me to get out of bed. "You can't keep this up. You've missed three weeks of school!"

I knew that's what she was supposed to say. I also knew that, if she didn't have to take Josey to preschool, she would've been in bed, too.

I'd heard her crying in the pantry more than once. Dad gave her the same speech about getting out of bed. Thankfully, some higher power pushed Dad to go on each day. *Someone* had to do the laundry, buy food, and cook. With an inner strength, Dad did it all and even went to work. Josey seemed to be getting along fine without Ben, but she was only four.

"Hannah, you've got to eat!" Her tapping turned to hammering.

"I'm not hungry," I hollered back, covering my head with my pillow.

"I'm coming in!"

The previous day, Dad had turned my doorknob around so I couldn't lock myself in again. It was insulting. *As if I didn't know where to find a screwdriver of my own and turn the doorknob back around.*

Mom came in my room and dropped down on the bed. She sniffed the air, groaned, and ripped the covers and pillow off me.

"You need a shower!"

"No!" I covered my face with my arms. "Leave me alone!"

Mom pulled them away and held them to my sides. I turned my head away.

She turned my chin toward her. "Oh, my god, what did you do?"

I snapped my head away.

"What happened to your eyelashes?"

I covered my face again.

She scrutinized the small pile of eyelashes on my night table.

"Why did you do that?"

Mom put her hands under my arms and lifted me off the bed. I went limp. She dragged me to the bathroom. When my feet hit the cold tile, I kicked and screamed.

"Leave me alone! I'm tired! I need to sleep!"

She lugged me across the stinging floor and tried to pull off my pajama bottoms.

"Quit it!"

Out of breath from trying to wrestle me out of my pj's, she shouted, "You've got to stop this! You can't stay in bed forever!"

I went limp again as she shoved me into the shower.

"Stop it! It's cold! It hurts!"

I backed into the corner of the shower and my screams morphed into wails.

The water started to warm up. Then I felt her hand on my forehead brushing the hair out of my face.

I opened my eyes.

Mom was next to me, fully clothed, in the shower, crying, too.

"I know. I'm tired too," she said. "But we can't sleep anymore. We have to move forward."

Mom put shampoo in my hair and lathered it up. I remained still while she pulled down the shower hose and rinsed the shampoo away. I felt like I was four years old again.

Safe.

Loved.

Protected.

By the end of the afternoon, we were in some counselor's office and I was in "therapy."

12

HANK

WEDNESDAY

The use of middle names originated during the Middle Ages in Europe. Some amateur forensic scientists are quick to point out that lone gunmen, like Lee Harvey Oswald, John Wilkes Booth, and James Earl Ray, tend to be identified by all three of their names; while serial killers are often identified using only their first and last names, like Jeffrey Dahmer and Ted Bundy. Obvious exceptions are John Wayne Gacy, AKA the "Clown Killer," and Joseph James Angelo, the "Golden State Killer." See Forensics 411 *episode 36, "What's In A Name?"*

THAT WEDNESDAY, we had a substitute in biology. It was Mr. Blackburn, one of those grumpy older people who must've discovered that retirement didn't pay as well as he thought it would.

He was calling out everyone's full name.

"Henry Amad Boyd?" Mr. Blackburn said, surveying the room for who might possibly fit that name. It was as if he hadn't subbed in every school in our repressively small district for years and come across my name scores of times.

I raised my hand. "Um, it's Henry *Adam* Boyd, and I go by Hank."

"Are you sure?" He repositioned his reading glasses. "It says A-M-A-D here."

"Yes," I answered. "It was a typo on my birth certificate. My mother has never been able to straighten it out."

I wasn't sure if she'd ever tried. It's not like we talked about anything related to my birth or the certification thereof. That was a topic involving my paternity and we kept that, through our mutual silence, comfortably behind the secret door to her secret past with my secret (or possibly unknown) father.

"Well, you better get on that or it's going to be a real challenge to collect social security."

"Yes, sir." *I'll see what I can do over the next fifty years.*

AFTER SCHOOL, Katelyn had band practice, but Hannah and I rode our bikes to the boatyard with the hope of questioning Old Man Fripp. We checked in with Mr. Phil first.

"Do you think Mr. Fripp will talk to us today?"

"Only if you have a death wish," Mr. Phil said. "His mood is even worse than yesterday! He's been calling the boat owners, and several have said they're no longer going to store their boats here. We're only at about fifty-percent capacity to begin with, so Grady can't really afford to lose any customers."

"I guess we'll try again tomorrow," I said.

AT HOME, Chaucer stood at the fence in the backyard wagging his tail with heart-warming enthusiasm.

"Hey boy!" I opened the gate so he could come up the back steps onto the porch. "How was your day?" I perched myself on the top step.

He lay next to me and thumped his tail against the deck.

"Glad to hear it," I said, running my hands over his long, soft ears. He leaned into me, so I didn't have to reach so far.

The screen door into the kitchen creaked open, and Grandpa said, "Frank, I didn't know you were out here."

"It's Hank, not Frank."

"I know. I like to pull your leg."

I stood up. "Do you really think you should make jokes about your dementia? That's kind of sick."

Grandpa held the door open for me and Chaucer. "Well, I am losing it!" He cackled.

"Seriously, Grandpa, it's not funny!"

"Boomer—and yes I know you're going by Hank these days —but I'm going to call you Boomer, because whether we like it or not, my memory *is* failing me. I'm going to joke about it for as long as I can. How was school?"

I grunted.

"What happened?"

"Everything."

"You didn't talk about your murder movies, did you?"

"My webisodes are about *all* crime, not just murder. They focus on the science behind solving crimes. Forensics can be used to solve robberies, bombings, rapes, and kidnappings... all kinds of good stuff."

"Good stuff?" Grandpa shook his head. "That's the worst mess that could happen to a person."

"I know. But solving the crimes holds the culprits responsible and gets justice for the victims. That's the power of forensics. It's important."

Grandpa and I sat at the table for our usual after-school snack.

Reflecting on what had happened in biology class, I asked, "Is your middle name Adam?"

"No," he answered through a cracker he'd just shoved in his mouth. "Why?"

"Well, I assumed I'm named after you since we're both Henrys. What's your middle name?"

"James."

"Henry James Boyd?"

"Yep."

"Then who's Adam?"

"Adam?" Grandpa closed the cracker box and walked it over to the sink. "That's the fella that's married to Eve."

"Not him! My middle name. Who am I named after?" I asked while casually putting the crackers in the pantry.

"I know I'm losing my mind, but your middle name isn't Adam; it's Amad." His expression brightened. "Hey, that's one of those anagrams you were telling me about—same letters, but in a different order."

My stomach dropped to the floor.

"Who's *Amad*?"

"I've always assumed he was your father since you came out browner than the rest of us."

Grandpa laughed at his off-color joke.

"You know who my father is?"

"Of course," Grandpa said. "This isn't one of those TV shows where women have to get paternity tests to know who the father of their baby is. Your mama's better than that!"

"Are you kidding me?" I said. "All these years you thought— no *assumed*—that I knew who my father was even though I never talked about him?"

"Don't you get sassy with me! You never asked me about him, so how was I supposed to know that you didn't know who he was. You've always been curiouser than a three-legged dog at a Chinese restaurant, so I figured you knew."

"Did you ever meet him?"

"Just once, when Angela graduated from college. They got an apartment together, then, next thing we knew, he got deported and your mama's pregnant."

"Deported?"

My mind raced. I had a father named Amad, not Adam. He and Mom had been *engaged,* then he got kicked out of the country.

"Why was he deported?"

Grandpa stared out the kitchen window for a second. "I think that was on account of him being a terrorist."

My mouth fell open.

"My father was a *terrorist?* Mom was engaged to a terrorist? And his name was Amad?"

Grandpa backed up.

"Um, I shouldn't have said anything. Don't tell your mama— she'll kill me!"

I paced around the kitchen. "How? How could you keep this from me my whole life?"

Grandpa shrugged. "I swear, I didn't know you didn't know. Angela never specifically told me not to tell you about him. I figured you knew and didn't want to talk about it because you were embarrassed—and she was too, I think. I mean, would you want to have to carry that around with you your whole life— that your dad was a terrorist?"

Grandpa stepped toward me with his hands in the air. "No more questions! I shouldn't have said anything. It's this damn dementia! I don't know what I'm saying half the time. Your father wasn't a terrorist. He was a teacher who just so happened to come from one of those places over there in the mountains that breed terrorists and goats."

With his words, I imagined the buffet of stereotypical nick-names Dillon would pin on me: Boomer bin Laden, Hank Hussein, Boomer the Bomber, Hank the Hijacker. The possibilities were endless.

"Tell me everything you know."

"Everything he knows about what?" my mom said as she came through the back door and set her briefcase on the counter.

"About my father the terrorist!" I cried, barreling past her and out the back door.

As the screen door slammed behind me, I heard Mom bellow, "Dad!"

13

HANNAH

C ockamamie *(adj.) ridiculous, implausible*

"Hannah!"

"What?"

"Hank's here."

"Send him up." It was an opportune time because I was stuck on a word problem. I really had no idea why I needed to be able to calculate the difference in the arrival time of two trains traveling at two different speeds to two different train stations. First of all, I never traveled by train, and second, that's what they had train schedules for.

Mom escorted Hank upstairs and made a big show of pushing my door open as wide as it would go. I thought the doorknob might go straight through the wall.

"What's up?"

"*What's up!*" he repeated erratically, sitting down on my bed, and then immediately popping back up and pacing.

"I'll tell you what's up!" he growled. "My father, *Amad,* —yes, that's right A-M-A-D, *not* A-D-A-M—is a freaking terrorist! I'm the spawn of Osama bin Laden and Saddam Hussein mixed up into one creepy little, twin-towers-bombing terrorist!"

"What?"

"My grandfather just told me. He thought I knew. *Amad* and my mom were engaged, but then he got deported because of his status as a terrorist."

I giggled.

"It's not funny!"

"Okay, tell me, where is your father from? Is he alive? Does your mom keep in touch with him?"

"According to Grandpa, he's from the place with all the terrorists and goats."

"Oh ya, that's next to the place with all the Black people and lions! My grandfather's people are from there!" She clucked her tongue in judgment.

"Hannah—focus! My father is a terrorist!"

"Your grandfather has dementia. He could be completely wrong."

Hank trudged to my dresser and examined himself in the mirror. "It would explain my uni-brow and abundant leg hair."

"*What*?" I asked.

"Armenians, Kurds, Afghans, Iranians, Pakistanis, Iraqis—they tend to be hairy."

"What are you talking about?"

"I was curious whether there is a correlation between quantity of body hair and the propensity to commit crime."

"So, you think that hairier people commit more crimes?" I asked. "Or were you wondering whether they just got caught more often because they tend to shed at the crime scene? Is that *seriously* what you sit around and think about?"

"It turns out those hairy countries don't publish their crime statistics; therefore, I wasn't able to draw any conclusions."

"Hairy countries?" I laughed. "It's official—you've lost it."

"Seriously! Focus!" He fell backwards across my bed. "My father is a terrorist!"

"*Because his legs are hairy?*" I laughed harder. "Or because *your* legs are hairy?"

He rolled onto his stomach and threw his arms over the side of the bed. "No, I'm hairy because of the Middle Eastern blood coursing through my veins."

"Okay, just stop! You're getting yourself all worked up over nothing. You need to talk to your mom. Get the facts, not the stereotypes. She'll tell you the truth. And she'll certainly want to set you straight if you go to her with this cockamamie story about your father being a hairy terrorist—that's a tongue twister. Let's just call him a *hairorist* for short!"

Hank rolled onto his back, this time draping his long arms across his forehead. "Not humorous!"

He sat up. "Do you realize what I'll have to endure at school if anyone finds out about this? You can't tell anyone!"

"Puhleaze—like I want to be known as bin Laden's bestie!"

He curled his lip at me. "Also, non-funny."

I stood up and yanked him off my bed. "Come on! We can stay here and exchange racist clichés all day, or we can find out the truth. What time does your mom get home from work?"

"She's already home."

"Okay, then you need to talk to her." I pushed him toward my doorway.

"Will you come with me?" His head hung forward.

"Dude, as much as I'd like to be a fly on the wall when you ask your mom whether your father is a terrorist, I think it might be awkward for me to lurk."

Hank ran his hand through his hair.

I squeezed his shoulder. "Good luck. And *do* call me as soon as you talk to her. I may be polite, but my curiosity is piqued."

14

HANK

The term broken home was first used in the mid-1800s to describe the absence of one parent for reasons such as prolonged illness, death, divorce, incarceration, or desertion. The preferred term today is single-parent household. *For decades, sociologists have searched for proof that being raised by only one parent leads to juvenile delinquency, but research has been inconclusive. See* Forensics 411 *episode 33, "Broken Homes, Broken Laws?"*

MOM WAS WAITING for me at the kitchen table with a large book sitting in front of her. I could tell by the expression on her face that she had talked to Grandpa.

"Come." She tapped the seat next to her. "Sit. We need to talk."

It made me furious how calm she was.

She took a deep breath. "I loved your father and he loved me. And he was *not* a terrorist."

"But Grandpa—"

"Stop." She raised her hand. "You are going to let me talk without interruptions."

"But—"

"Nope—no interruptions. Not one. Not even a tiny one."

Mom opened the large book. It was a photo album I'd never seen before. Turning it so I could see, she pointed, "This is your father. His name was Amad Khalud. He was getting his PhD when I met him my sophomore year of college. I was nineteen. He was twenty-four."

In the photo, Mom stood next to a tall, thin man with dark wavy hair. He had dimples just like me, though I only had one. He was nearly a foot taller than her. His long straight nose was mine. His skin color was mine. Though my eyes were lighter, the picture could have been me in another ten years.

"He was born in Kabul, Afghanistan. His father worked for the government. Amad was incredibly bright." She patted my arm. "That's where you get your brains. The Soviet Union invaded Afghanistan in late 1979, and Amad was born just a couple months later. The war lasted ten years. Millions fled the country, mostly to Iran or Pakistan. Because of his position in the government, Amad's father was able to send Amad, his mother, and sister to London for the entire war. His mother and sister returned to Kabul in the early nineties, but Amad stayed in London through college, then he came to UNC for his PhD in Mathematics."

She turned the page to another picture of the two of them.

"He taught my Calculus class." Mom grinned. "I went to his office for help one day and we just got to talking. He was smart, funny, and handsome." Mom touched my cheek. "Just like you."

"He proposed to me a few months before I graduated. His father didn't approve because I was American and not Muslim. Having grown up away from Afghanistan, Amad was not devout. His father thought he became too *westernized*." Mom shook her head. "I don't know what his father had expected to happen. *He'd* been the one to send his wife and children to the UK."

She flipped the page of the album. "The 9/11 terrorist attacks happened when I was in college. Then we invaded Iraq. Some

Americans became anti-Muslim, anti-Arab and especially anti-Afghan—though none of the terrorists that attacked us even came from Afghanistan. When his student visa expired in early 2005, he had to go back to Afghanistan to renew it. I begged him not to go." She touched the photo. "He lived in Afghanistan when he was a tiny baby and had only visited a few times." Mom stared at the kitchen wall. "I never understood why he didn't just become a British citizen."

A tear rolled down her cheek. "When he had to return to Afghanistan to renew his visa, I was afraid he wouldn't be able to get back to the US."

She pointed to a photo of her in cap and gown. "Shortly after he left, I found out I was pregnant with you. I wrote him but received a letter from his father telling me that Amad had been killed by a roadside bomb. He told me to never write again." Mom's voice choked up. "So, Amad never knew about you."

"Grandpa said he got deported because he was a terrorist."

Mom shook her head. "Sweetie, he didn't even get deported. He just had to return to Kabul to renew his student visa at a very anti-Muslim, anti-Afghan time in our country. Even though, like I said, he didn't even practice Islam and he lived most of his life in London."

"Did he have a British accent?"

Mom smiled. "Yes. I used to love it when he said things like 'trousers' and 'cheers.'"

"Does Grandpa know he wasn't a terrorist?" I asked.

"Yes. You know Grandpa—he just says things. He only met Amad once."

She turned the page and showed me another picture from her college graduation. "See the expression on Dad's face? This is right after we told my parents we were getting married."

"What about Grandma? Did she like him?"

"Neither one of them got a chance to know him before he had to return to Kabul."

"Were you happy when you found out you were pregnant?"

"I was scared. I was only twenty-one—didn't know how my parents would react. My fiancé was away in a country that was in the middle of a war with the United States. Obviously, it wasn't an ideal situation. But I loved Amad. He was a good man. And with how things ended up, it turned out to be a blessing that I got pregnant. I have a little piece of him in my heart but an even bigger piece of him in you."

"So, you weren't humiliated to have an illegitimate child?"

Mom shook her head. "It wasn't the 1940s. I mean, my parents weren't thrilled that I got pregnant when I wasn't married, but I didn't have to 'go stay with an aunt in Oklahoma' like they did in the old days. Amad and I had an apartment in Chapel Hill. The lease ran out a few months before my due date. At that point, I came home to stay with my parents... and obviously, I never left."

In all the years I had tried to imagine what my father was like and why he had abandoned me and Mom, this had *never* been part of the scenario.

"Wow. He wasn't some sleezebag guy who was married, or a criminal, or somebody you made a mistake with?"

"No. He loved me, and though he never got the chance to know about you, I guarantee he would've been happy and proud to be your father. And never, *ever* have I considered him or you a mistake."

"Then why didn't you put his name on my birth certificate?" I asked.

"You know about that?"

"Yes."

"I was young, immature, and afraid because he was Afghan. It wasn't a good time to be from that part of the world. I didn't want you to have to deal with the countless questions and assumptions people were making after 9/11. I didn't want to put that weight on your shoulders at such a young age."

I pulled the photo album closer and flipped through the

pages. "Is that why you let me think my middle name was Adam instead of Amad?"

She nodded.

"Are there more pictures of him?"

"Uh-huh," she said. "There's one back here of the last time we were together. It was taken at the airport in Raleigh when he was on his way to Kabul."

I leaned closer.

"I look just like him."

Mom wrapped her arms around me. "Yes, you do."

"Did you tell his family when I was born?"

"No. Amad's father was *very* clear in his letter that I should never contact him or his family again."

"Do you mind if I take this album in my room and look at it some more?"

"Of course not."

I stood up.

"Sweetie?"

"Yeah?" I turned to look at her.

"I'm sorry. We should've had this conversation a long time ago. That was stupid of me."

"Yeah."

"Forgive me?"

I swallowed hard, then nodded.

In my room, I collapsed onto my bed with the photo album and dialed Hannah.

15

HANNAH

P *rogeny (n.) descendent, child, offspring*

HANK WAS SITTING on his bed reading something on his phone when I tapped on the window.

He opened it, saying, "Hey. Thanks for coming. We have doors, you know."

"I know. I just didn't know what the climate was going to be with your mom." I catapulted myself hands and head-first through the window and onto his bed.

"What's the deal? *Is* the hairorist a terrorist?"

"No, it's nothing like that. My father's name was Amad Khalud. He was born in Afghanistan but lived most of his life in London." He turned a photo album toward me. "This is him."

"Holy cow! You look just like him!"

"His father worked for the government. After the Soviet Union invaded Afghanistan in late 1979, he sent his wife, my dad, and my dad's sister to live in London. Apparently, I have an aunt."

I studied the photo album while Hank recounted the story of his father's life.

"So, you're the progeny of a tragic love story?" I fell backwards onto his bed. "That's so romantic."

"Before you start writing a made-for-TV movie, there's more. Look what I got a few minutes ago." He showed me the screen of his phone.

"Ooh, *MyDNAHistory.com*—your test results?"

"Yep. I used the hundred bucks from Mrs. McFarland to pay for it."

"May I?"

I took the phone from him and clicked on *View Your Reports*.

"Okay," I read aloud. "European—fifty-three-point-six percent. That's broken down into British and Irish forty-point-two percent; French and German seven-point-nine percent, Eastern European five-point-five percent."

"That's my mom's side," Hank said.

"No Scandinavian blood? You poor thing. The Swedes are a hardy stock."

"Believe me, Scotland doesn't turn out a bunch of softies," Hank said. "The Boyd clan fought off English invaders for generations. And the weather there positively sucks."

I scrolled down. "Okay, this sounds like your father's people, *Broadly Central Asian, Northern Indian and Pakistani.*"

I clicked on that and read aloud: "Because of the southward migration of people from Central Asia about four thousand years ago, the people of Central Asia, Northern India and Pakistan have a shared genetic heritage which makes it difficult to assign some DNA to just one group."

Next, I clicked on *Central Asia* and read the list of countries: Afghanistan, Kazakhstan, Kyrgyzstan, Tajikistan, Turkmenistan, Uzbekistan. Hank's largest percentage of those subgroups was Afghan.

"Dude, you are most definitely *not* Greek or Italian."

"Did you think I *was*?" Hank asked.

"Remember—over the summer when we were searching for Chaucer on the island—you told me your father was Mediterranean and that he died before you were born."

"I... well... I lied about that. Sorry. I had no idea what I was. But I was right about my dad being dead."

"Oh, no. Really?"

"Killed by some kind of roadside bomb."

"Jeez, I could turn this saga into a best seller," I lamented. "You know, if you consider the Scots rugged, you've got to give props to your Central Asian ancestors. They have huge mountains, deserts, and extreme weather, year-round. Your dad comes from some tough people."

"If anyone at school finds out about this, I doubt that the ruggedness of my ancestors will trump the stereotypes of Middle Easterners."

"Dude, chillax, look at your results. You're not 'Middle Eastern,' you're 'Broadly Central Asian.'" I used finger quotes.

"I'll be sure to throw that technicality at Dillon when he calls me a son-of-a-terrorist."

I nodded. "Yeah, the politically correct re-branding of that region hasn't been as successful as they hoped."

"The intellectually bankrupt will jump on any racist stereotype."

"I think you're guilty of that yourself," I said.

"I am?"

"Yes. *You're* the one aligning your Afghan heritage with terrorism."

"I *am?*"

"You are," I explained. "Are you going to start praying five times a day, write in Arabic, or expect women to be covered from head to toe because you found out your father was from Afghanistan?" I gawked at him. "No. You're the same forensics-loving weirdo you were yesterday. You just happen to know a bit more about your roots. If you choose, you can explore your father's culture. Experiment with it. Get yourself a *shalwar kameez* to cover those hairy legs of yours. See if you want to incorporate some of it into the Hank that the rest of the world sees."

"I guess," he mumbled. "What about you? Do you consider yourself more Black or more white?"

I shrugged. It was a question I'd been forced to contemplate many times. "For me, it seemed like before about second grade, kids didn't even notice race. Your friends were your friends—black, white, and brown. Then something seemed to happen. Around age eight, some light bulb clicks on in the child brain and they seem to realize that we aren't all actually the same. I guess it's just something in human nature that we need to sort people and objects. Maybe it all goes back to kindergarten when we had to look at objects on a piece of paper and circle which one didn't belong." I looked at him. "You know—cat, dog, mouse, tree."

I shrugged. "By middle school, I wasn't *black enough* for the Black kids. And honestly, I think most white people didn't even realize that I wasn't 'pure white'—if there's such a thing. I grew up with my parents and grandparents looking like they look. And acting like they act—as embarrassing as that sometimes is! They raised me to not feel like I have to choose one race over the other. But that's not how society as a whole works. "

Hank gave me a thoughtful look. "Are you saying that our heritage doesn't have to be our heritage if we don't want it to be?"

"No. That's not at all what I'm saying."

He stared at his wheezing window air conditioner. "I guess I've never felt like I quite belonged anywhere because I look so different from my mom and grandpa. Now I know where I *might* belong, and it's scary because of the negativity about that part of the world."

"Hank, the reason you feel like you don't belong anywhere is because *you don't*! And I mean that in the kindest possible way. You are unlike any creature I've ever met. You make videos about crime *for fun*! You think that boomeranging is an actual sport. You blink more in one day than most of us will blink in a lifetime. You *are* different from anyone else I've ever met, and it's not because your dad's from Central Asia or your grandpa has a kilt fetish; it's because you're peculiar!" I nudged him in the side with my elbow. "And trust me, I don't think that you'd blend in well in Kabul, either."

"Thanks," Hank said, gazing at me from under his wavy bangs. "But seriously, do you consider yourself more Black or more white?"

I thought about it.

"I guess, genetically, I'm seventy-five percent white and twenty-five percent Black, but that's just biology," I said. "Remember how you told me you'd never asked your mom about your father because you didn't want her to feel like she wasn't 'enough' as a parent? That's sort of how I feel about my race. It would be kind of disrespectful to one of my parents or grandparents if I decided to 'be Black' or 'be white,' as if there even is such a thing. Society wants to check a race box next to my name. *You* want to check a race box next to *your* name. But that box doesn't determine who you are as a person. You do."

I leaned against the wall. "Do you feel *complete* now that you know where the other half of your DNA came from?"

He shrugged his shoulders. "Not really. I guess I'm more confused than ever."

"Confusion is a by-product of thinking—a pit-stop on the road trip to realization and clarity. Think of it this way: the ignorant don't know enough to realize they should be confused."

"That's quite deep," Hank said.

I smiled. "You didn't know I was an intellectual giant?"

Someone knocked on the door.

"Should I hide?" I asked.

"Why would you hide?"

"If my mom saw a boy in my room that had not come through any of the doors, there would be some mama drama."

"Hank, are you okay?" his mom asked through the door. "I thought I heard voices."

"I'm fine. Just looking at the album you gave me."

"Can I come in?"

I frantically shook my head.

"Sure," he said.

I dove to the puke-green carpet behind his bed as she opened the door.

"*Hannah?*"

I peeked my head over the side of Hank's twin bed and said, "Oh, hi, Ms. Boyd."

"What are you doing here? It's almost eight o'clock."

Then she focused on the open bedroom window, and her eyes narrowed.

"Did you come through the window?"

"She did, Mom, but only because I asked her to. I just needed to talk to her."

His mom searched for signs that I secretly lived in Hank's room.

"This is the first time I've ever used the window as a point of entry," I said. "Hank just—like he said—needed a friend."

"Well, you should be heading home. I'm sure your parents are wondering where you are."

"Okay," I said glancing at the open window.

Ms. Boyd pointed. "You can use the door."

16

HANK
THURSDAY

The Oxford Dictionary *defines terrorism as the unlawful use of violence and intimidation, especially against civilians, in the pursuit of political aims. In recent years, the nations of the Philippines, Afghanistan, Iraq, Pakistan, India, and Somalia have had the most frequent incidents of terrorism. The world's deadliest terrorist attack took place in New York City on September 11, 2001 when 2,996 people were killed and more than 6,000 injured. See* Forensics 411 *episode 34, "Terrorism: It's Supposed to Scare You," for a more detailed look.*

THE NEXT MORNING, Hannah enthusiastically plopped down beside me on the bus, leaned over and whispered, "'Sup, slum dog?"

"Ha, ha, ha."

"What? No shoulder-launched missile today?"

"There will, *never*, not *ever*, be a time when terrorist jokes are funny or appropriate."

"Okay, fine," Hannah said, "but I'm working on something really good about skyjacking. It's your loss."

"Just stop."

Hannah snickered.

"I asked Dad. It turns out we did have insurance on our boat. If there were a word other than *nerdy* to describe my dad, it would be *judicious*."

"Judicious?" I said. "Like judgmental?"

Hannah rubbed her hands together as if she were cold. "Finally! A word you don't know!" Her hazel eyes sparkled. "Judicious means cautious, careful, well-advised. My dad does *not* like to be surprised. He plans everything. He researched boats for two years before he ordered the one that got stolen. He's judicious."

17

HANNAH

T *irade (n.) a long, angry speech of criticism or accusation*

HANK CALLED me after school with a "job." In his world, *job* meant he would be bossing me around and neither of us would get paid.

"So, basically we go door to door and ask people if they saw or heard anything the night of the robbery?" I said.

"Yes. You write their names, addresses and answers in our case notebook. It's possible someone was awake and saw or heard something before, during, or after the burglary."

"Clerical work? Is that because I'm *the girl*?"

"No," he said, "and don't even try to turn this into one of your women's liberation tirades. You just have better hand-writing."

"What about Katelyn? Is she going with us?"

"She has band practice today. Plus, Corker is only letting me help because I promised that you would be the only person I'd share the information with."

"*With whom* you'd share the information," I said.

"That's what I said."

"No, it wasn't. You ended your sentence with a preposition, which is a grammar *faux pas*." When Hank got to doling out assignments, I liked to remind him which of us had a superior command of the English language.

"Our interviews need to be on the down-low."

"When are we going to do these interviews?"

"Right now," he answered. "Grab your bike and meet me at the intersection between our houses."

WE STARTED with the house closest to the boatyard. A woman in her late twenties or early thirties answered the door with a baby strapped to her body in one of those carrier things. Her name was Leslie Davis.

Hank introduced himself and asked her the pertinent questions: Was she the homeowner? Was she home on Monday night/Tuesday morning when the robbery occurred? Did she see or hear anything? Did she have a boat stored at the marina?

Yes. Yes. Maybe. And no.

"I'm a light sleeper," Leslie explained while jiggling the baby. "He's three months old and eats every four hours. When I was feeding him on Monday night, my dog, Hugo, was out in the back yard going crazy. Once I heard about the robbery, I figured that Hugo must've seen the robbers and that's why he was barking so much."

"And what time was that?"

"Around two in the morning."

"Did you check on why he was being so loud?"

"I peeked out the back window and he was pacing and barking along the side of the fence closest to the marina. He does that sometimes if he sees a deer. The barking stopped after I went back to bed," she said. "But in the morning, I figured out that he had stopped barking because he was busy digging under the fence. Hugo can't do two things at once."

"Did he get out?" Hank asked.

"Yes."

"Can we meet your dog?"

"Sure," she said. "I've got him in his crate right now because my husband hasn't filled the hole back yet."

Mrs. Davis disappeared into the house and came back dragging a large white German Shepard by the collar, with the other hand supporting the baby.

"This is Hugo. He's been a bad boy!"

"Hi, Hugo," I said, putting my hand down so he could sniff it.

He jumped up and put his paws on my shoulders just like Chaucer liked to do.

"Down!"

"It's all right," I said pulling my head back to better examine Hugo. "You're a cutie! I've never seen a white one before."

"They're unique," Mrs. Davis said.

"It looks like he's got a little something on his neck," Hank said.

"Really? I thought I got it all off," she said. "I think it was blood."

"Did he have blood on him before he escaped the yard the night of the boatyard burglary?" Hank asked.

"No, he showed up the next morning with it."

Hank reached in his backpack and took out an army knife and a zipper bag. "I know this is an odd request, but do you mind if I take a sample? The police chief will want to do DNA testing on it."

She shrugged. "I guess not."

Hank put on latex gloves and cut the small brownish clump of fur out of Hugo's otherwise white neck.

"Do you always carry latex gloves and zipper bags with you?" I asked.

"Any place can turn into a crime scene in seconds," he explained. He turned to Mrs. Davis. "Does Hugo tend to bark at strangers?"

"Are there dogs that don't?" she answered and gave him a pat on the head. "He doesn't stand at the fence and bark at the people at the boat ramp all day, if that's what you mean. Most of the regulars know him by name, and he knows them. But if he saw people at the boat ramp at night, that would've set him off. The boat ramp closes at dusk."

"We'll send this off to the crime lab for analysis," Hank said.

"The police must really trust you kids," she said.

"Yes," Hank answered. "Has Hugo ever bitten anyone?"

"Never. The other night was the only time he's ever been outside the fence alone." She motioned with her head. "Come on, Hugo, in the house."

"Thank you, Mrs. Davis," Hank said. "Here's my card. Call, text, or email me if you think of anything else."

At the next house our English teacher, Mrs. Ozmore, answered the door.

"Hey, you two," she said with a smile. "To what do I owe this pleasure outside of school?"

"You live here?" Hank asked.

"I do."

"We're helping with the investigation into the robbery at Fripp's Boatyard on Monday night or early Tuesday morning."

"I heard about that. They stole the stereo system from my friend's boat."

"Really?" I asked. "What's her name?"

"Lacy Garfield," Mrs. Ozmore said. "Her husband owns an audio store in Wilmington, so you can imagine how nice that stereo was. They'd just started storing their boat at Fripp's."

She got a suspicious expression on her face. "Shouldn't the police be asking the questions?"

"As I said, Officer Steve Corker, the acting chief of police, asked for our help."

"He's Hank's mom's *boyfriend*," I interjected for the joy of watching Hank cringe.

In retaliation, he rubbed the top of my head, loosening the curls I tried to keep subdued in a ponytail and said pointedly, "He's a *family* friend."

"Did you hear about us solving the McFarland case this summer?" I asked.

"You guys were all over the news."

"We were the ones who re-opened that cold case," Hank said. "We brought the local cops and SBI in later when we had some leads."

That wasn't *exactly* how it happened, but I knew where he was headed.

"The interim chief is swamped with cases right now and asked us to interview possible witnesses," Hank said convincingly. "Did you see or hear anything unusual?"

"That was the first day of school, and I was wiped out. I was in bed by nine o'clock." She glanced in the direction of the marina. "One thing was kind of unusual. I went out to the mailbox after dinner, and a big truck—you know, an eighteen-wheeler—drove by. It was going pretty fast. We don't get many big trucks down here because the road is a dead end."

"What did it look like?"

"Big. Red. Squeaky brakes."

"Did you see the driver?" Hank asked.

Mrs. Ozmore shook her head.

"And what time was that?"

"Eight or eight-thirty."

"And did you see where the truck went?" I asked.

"It stopped at the boatyard gate. It didn't have a choice. The gate was closed. The driver honked his horn a couple times like he was expecting someone to come open the gate for him."

"Did anyone open it?" Hank asked.

"Not that I saw."

"Was the truck there in the morning?"

"Not that I remember."

"And you never heard the truck go by in the middle of the night?" I asked.

"No. Like I said, I was exhausted that night. The first day of school always kills me. I slept like a log."

Hank handed her his card. "If you think of anything else, call, email, or text me."

She smiled. "Or I could just talk to you in first period."

"Oh, sure," Hank said. "That'll work, too."

At the next house, a leathery woman in her sixties answered the door with an unfriendly, "What do you want?"

She wore a black t-shirt that said *I DON'T CARE ABOUT YOUR FEELINGS!* and I believed her.

"Hi, I'm Hank Boyd and this is Hannah Simmons. The police chief, Steve Corker—"

She wagged her finger at us. "Oh, I know who you are! You're the ones to blame for the robbery!"

"What?" Hank said.

"My husband and I built that boatyard and marina from the ground up."

"You're Mrs. Fripp?" I asked.

"Who'd you think I was?" she said. "In forty years, we've never had so much as a trespasser, then y'all get Chester Buckley fired, and we get robbed! That ain't a coincidence!"

Hank and I made eye contact, knowing that *we* had trespassed on the property more than once over the summer.

"It's not our fault," I argued. "My family's brand-new boat was taken because all you have is a padlock and chain on a gate that is supposed to protect hundreds of thousands—if not millions—of dollar's-worth of boats."

Hank whispered, "Down girl."

I didn't back down. "Maybe if your husband put fresh

batteries in the security cameras, the cops would've caught the thieves already!"

Mrs. Fripp jerked back as if I'd slapped her in the face.

"We constantly rotate those cameras through the charger."

"They have *rechargeable* batteries?" Hank asked.

"Of course," she barked. "We have two extra cameras, so when the boys take one down to charge, they put a fully charged one back in that spot, and we have a spare just in case something goes wrong. We have them staggered so that no two cameras go dead at the same time. It's what the man at the store said to do. I made a schedule, so the boys know which camera needs to be checked in the rotation each week. The charge in the cameras is supposed to last three months but each camera gets a fresh charge every five weeks."

It sounded as if Mrs. Fripp was way more organized that Mr. Fripp.

"So, you have five cameras?" I asked.

"Six. Two at the dock, one at the gate, one outside, and one inside the store. The sixth one is in the shop and our mechanic keeps that one charged."

"Did someone order cameras for the dry stack areas?" Hank asked.

"Emmitt did, but they're on backorder."

"Well, thank you for your help, ma'am."

"You're not welcome!" she said, slamming the door in our faces.

We picked up our bikes and moved to the next house.

"She's charming," I said.

"Check it out!" Hank said, pointing to the doorbell at the neighboring house. "It's one of those video doorbells!"

The owner of the next house was Eugene Lund, a man in his seventies with thin gray hair and lonely blue eyes.

In his explanation to Mr. Lund about why we were there, Hank made us sound like we'd been deputized by God herself to investigate the robbery.

"Sir, we were wondering if you saw or heard anything interesting this past Monday or early Tuesday morning when the boatyard was burglarized."

"Can't say I did. What time are you curious about?"

"Your neighbor told us she saw an eighteen-wheeler go up the road toward the marina and that a large truck like that on this road was unusual."

"Very unusual," Mr. Lund said. "Since the road dead ends at the marina, if you take a semi up that way, it'd be a real challenge to get it back out. You ever done a three-point turn in an eighteen-wheeler?"

"No, sir."

"I used to be a truck driver. It's not easy to maneuver a truck like that."

"Did you see or hear the truck?"

"No. But I take my hearing aid out when I go to sleep. My daughter says I shouldn't do that, in case someone breaks in. That's why she got me that doorbell thingy. She gets an alert on her phone when someone comes to my door. I'm surprised she hasn't already called to find out who you kids are." He shook his head.

"How does your video doorbell work?" Hank asked.

"I don't really know. Somehow that thing knows when someone's on the porch. The camera just pops on. It's like magic."

Hank chuckled. "It has a motion sensor."

"The technology these days is just too much to keep up with. I never advanced past the CB radio in my truck."

"Do walkers or cars driving by trigger the camera?"

"Yes. Anytime someone goes by the house it clicks three times."

"And you said your daughter gets a notification on her phone. Does she get the video also?"

"The pictures go to the computer she made me get. At first, I couldn't imagine why I'd need a computer for anything. But shoot, I spend half my day online playing chess and the other half playing solitaire. It's like computers were invented for lonely widowers like me."

"It would really help our investigation if we could review the footage from your video doorbell and see if it caught anything related to the robbery."

"Sure. Come on in," he said, opening the door wider and leading us into his living room.

"I remember you kids from the paper this summer," he said. "My daughter and Stacy McFarland were in the same grade. They did Brownies and Girl Scouts together, too. The whole town was torn up when that girl disappeared."

"Yes, sir."

"Here's the computer."

The Lund house smelled like instant coffee, vanilla air fresheners, and moth balls. The television was on, and something about Mr. Lund told me that it was on most of the time. The counter was covered with dirty dishes, and the carpet, worn thin in many places, was an unusual shade of pink.

"May I sit?" Hank asked with manners I'd never seen him display.

"Sure." He pointed to the top left of the screen. "There's the little button for the doorbell camera."

Hank clicked on it.

"I need the password," Hank said.

"Rosie64," he said. "That's R-O-S-I-E-six-four in all capital letters. That's my late wife's name and the year we got married."

Mr. Lund seemed so sad I wanted to give him a hug.

Hank accessed the video file, and within minutes, had very brief video shots of the red truck going east toward the boatyard at 8:39 that evening and then passing Mr. Lund's house as it left at 2:20 the next morning.

"Mr. Lund," Hank said, "I know this video is not clear but, with your background as a truck driver, is there anything you could tell me about this truck?"

"Can I sit?" he asked Hank.

Hank moved out of the seat, and Mr. Lund put on a pair of half-moon glasses.

After a few moments of studying the picture, he whistled. "She's a beauty!"

"Can you tell the brand?"

"I'd have to see the grill of the truck for that." He pointed to the screen. "You see how this cab is flat in the front? That's called a cabover. That's what I started out driving back in the sixties. You don't see them around much in the United States, but they're still used over in Europe where they have stricter length laws for trucks."

"What makes it a *cabover*?"

"The cab of the truck, where the driver sits and sleeps, is *above* the motor. It doesn't make for the most comfortable ride, and it was a real challenge to get in and out because there wasn't good footing," he said with a nostalgic smile. "Up until 1976, the length of an eighteen-wheeler could only be sixty-five feet. The cabover saved on overall length of the truck so that the trailer could be longer. The longer the trailer, the more cargo the truck can haul, which means more income. In '76 they changed the laws, allowing for the overall length of trucks to be seventy-five feet, so the advantage of a cabover style disappeared. They're a real gem for collectors to restore."

He pointed to the screen. "But that thing doesn't look like it's been restored. It's got a lot of rust."

"What about the trailer?" Hank asked. "Can you tell us anything about that?"

Mr. Lund leaned in closer to the screen. "It's a flatbed with a fifty-five-foot storage container on it. I can't make out the name on the container."

"So, the part of the truck where stuff is stored isn't actually part of the truck?" I asked.

"No, the container is portable," he said. "A country like China exports all kinds of goods to America. The Chinese manufacturer loads its products into a shipping container in China, puts it on a cargo carrier, and delivers it to a port on the west coast. That shipping container might have goods meant for North Carolina, so rather than take everything out of one container and put it in another, the folks at the port take the entire container off the cargo ship with a crane, put it on the back of a flatbed truck or a train, and send it on its way to us in Wilmington, or Raleigh, or Charlotte. The container is emptied at its destination, then that empty container can be rented by someone else to transport *their* goods."

"Therefore, if I see a truck on the highway hauling a shipping container with Chinese writing on it, it might not have actually *just* come from China?"

"Right," Eugene Lund said. "That shipping container might've originally transported toys from China to America fifteen years ago, but once it got over here, it's been repeatedly rented by American businesses to transport their goods."

"Can anyone rent a shipping container?" I asked.

"Sure. A lot of businesses find it easier to rent the trailer and container than to own their own fleet of box trucks. That's what people in the shipping business call a flatbed trailer with a container on it."

"What about the truck itself—can you rent those?" I asked.

"You have to have a commercial driver's license to rent an eighteen-wheeler or a cab that's considered 'heavy duty.' But anyone can rent a smaller two-axle truck with a gross weight under 10,000 pounds."

Mr. Lund stood back up, and Hank sat down at the computer. He took screen shots of every vehicle and person that passed between Monday morning and the close of business on Tuesday.

"Mr. Lund, thank you so much for letting us see the videos. Here's my card. Please call me if you think of anything that could be related to the robbery at the boatyard."

"Did they steal boats?" Mr. Lund asked.

"One boat, several engines and a lot of electronics," Hank said. "Didn't Mr. Fripp tell you what was taken?"

"I haven't even seen him since it happened," he said. "It's a shame. Grady wanted to build those dry stacks for years. That was his dream. He put every cent he had into them, and then to turn around and get robbed? It's terrible!"

18

HANK

*A*n eyewitness is a person who directly sees an event occur; especially one who testifies about what he or she has seen. The less-familiar term "earwitness" is used to describe a person who testifies about an event that he or she directly heard. When a witness or victim of a crime hears but doesn't see a perpetrator, police use earwitness lineups or "voice parades" to help identify suspects. The witness is asked to listen to voice samples and make judgments about the perpetrator's identity based on what they hear. See Forensics 411 episode 30, "Do You Hear What I Hear?" for more about ear witnesses.

FOR THE SECOND day in a row, Corker was in the kitchen when I got back home. It was not a routine I was interested in establishing.

"Can Hannah stay for dinner?" I asked Mom. "We have a project for Biology to work on."

"Sure," Mom said. "We're going to eat in a few minutes so add another place at the table."

I went into the den, made a photocopy of the first page of our interview notes, and handed them to Corker.

I whispered, "Leslie Davis, who lives in the house closest to the boatyard, seemed to have some helpful information." I presented him with the zipper bag of Hugo's fur and explained his escape the night of the burglary.

"This could be the dog's own blood, but I didn't see any kind of wounds on him. I think he dug under the fence and may have attacked one of the burglars at the boatyard," I said. "Can you send this to the crime lab to be tested?"

"Didn't we already discuss that fact that I can't afford DNA testing? Buckley spent all the department's money. We're broke."

"Yes. But what if that thousand-dollar test gave you the answer to who stole hundreds of thousands of dollar's-worth of engines, boats and electronics?"

Corker peered at the plastic bag. "You really think this is thief blood?"

"Yes."

Where did the man come up with phrases like "thief blood?" Was that the terminology they taught at his backwoods police academy?

"Okay, I'll send this *one* thing off to the crime lab, but then that's it—no more!"

"Deal." I explained about Mrs. Ozmore seeing the red truck but didn't tell him about the video doorbell. "How much would it cost to track down the truck?"

"I've got to have more to go on than just that it's a red eighteen-wheeler with squeaky brakes," Corker said. "I need a license plate or a USDOT number from the truck cab."

"What about the cameras they have on the interstate signs? Or weigh stations—don't they take pictures of all the trucks that get weighed?"

"Yes, but it would be impossible to search all the highway video for every red tractor-trailer that passed. North Carolina doesn't even require all trucks to stop at weigh stations anymore." Corker shifted in his seat. "Do you know anything else about it besides the color?"

"It's an old-school cab with a flatbed trailer carrying a red shipping container."

"Get me more information and I'll see what I can do," Corker said. Then he leaned closer and said, "I emailed Cantrell's photos. Don't say anything to your mom."

AFTER DINNER, Hannah and I planted ourselves on the floor in front of my bed, with Chaucer between us.

I heard Mom griping at Corker in the kitchen. "I told you I don't want him involved in any more of your cases."

"It doesn't seem like there's anything of consequence in those pictures, but you never know. Hank notices things the rest of us don't."

I smiled, glad to know he appreciated my investigative instincts.

"Besides," Steve added, "it'll keep him busy and out of my hair."

"Why didn't you tell him about the video doorbell?" Hannah asked.

"To prove that I'm a better investigator than him."

"Don't we need him on our side to have access to the crime lab and all the databases?"

"Possibly," I said. "I'm going to see if Hacktivist77 can clean up the picture of the red truck so we can get a license plate or that USDOT number Corker said should be on the cab. He might also be able to tell us what the shipping container says so we could track down who rented it or where it was rented from."

"From where it was rented," Hannah said.

I ignored her attempt to be the Grammar Gestapo.

First, I messaged Hacktivist77 through my *Forensics 411* website. He was a regular poster who had helped us out with a phone tap during the McFarland case.

"How much is Hacktivist77 going to cost me this time?" Hannah asked.

If I was the brains of our operation, Hannah was the one who bankrolled most of our expenses.

"I'm sure he'll give us his best price," I said. "And I still have some money on that debit card we used for the tap on Chester Buckley's phone."

I logged into my email account on her laptop so we could watch the security video. "Let's get started."

19

HANNAH

Discrepancy *(n.) a lack of agreement between two or more facts, inconsistency*

WE WATCHED the boat shop security video first.

"It looks like Officer Cantrell cut the video footage down to just when the thieves were in the shop in the middle of the night," Hank said.

"Or maybe the camera is motion-activated."

Hank turned to me with a serious expression on his face. I prepared myself for one of his verbal ambushes about some episode of *Forensics 411* that I needed to watch about motion-activated technology, but instead, he said, "I bet you're right," and smiled at me. It was surreal.

The camera was positioned so it showed a wide angle of the shop. The time stamp said 2:07 when someone opened the center bay door of the shop. One masked person of medium build could be seen looking at the boxes of equipment stored on shelves, and a second masked person climbed on the boat closest to the camera, cut out the electronics in seconds, placed them in a wheelbarrow or dock cart, then exited the bay door.

"That's why I think these people are professionals. The guy at the shelves could've easily taken everything, but he's picking and choosing... and doing it quickly. Jeez, I wish we could zoom in on the video to see what equipment he took."

"Katelyn's dad can tell us that once he's done his inventory," I said.

Hank nodded. "WhoDunnitHannah is on the ball today!"

At 2:09, the second masked thief came back in the shop, pulled the engine hoist out through the central bay door, and disappeared off the screen.

I leaned in closer to the screen. "Go back."

"To where?"

"Back to when the guy who left the shop comes back in to get the engine hoist."

"Okay," Hank said, then cleared his throat. "But... um... uh..."

"Would you like to buy a consonant to go with that vowel?" I saw the distress in his eyes. "Do you need me to back away?"

He nodded.

I leaned back against the bed and scooted a few inches away.

"Look at his hand," I said. "Doesn't that look like he's holding a cigarette?"

"Yes!" Hank said. "Make a note that we need to search the area around the shop for cigarette butts. They'll have the smoker's DNA."

"But it's Thursday. How many people have been in the shop, the parking lot and near the dry stacks since the robbery? I would guess that more than one of them was a smoker."

"Maybe. But customers don't go in the fenced area to get their boat. They call the marina ahead of time, then Emmitt or Brock gets their boat for them and lowers it down into the water near the fuel dock."

"You're saying only people that work at the boatyard or burglarize it would go in the fenced area?"

"Yes."

"My whole family was in the fenced area on Monday!"

Hank slumped against the bed. "Good point."

"We can still check with Mr. Calhoun—see which employees smoke, or if he's seen any smoking customers there recently."

Hank took out his phone and typed.

"I texted Katelyn and asked her to ask her father our smoking question."

"Good," I said. "The lady with the baby—"

Hank's phone buzzed.

"I bet it's `Hacktivist77`." He put the phone on speaker and said, "Hello."

A computerized voice said, "What's up, 411?"

"I have a screenshot from a doorbell video. It's grainy. There's a tractor-trailer, and we need to know if there's anything written on the cab, and if so, what it says. Also, can you read the word written on the trailer part of the truck and clean the photo up enough to see the license plate?"

The creepy computer voice said, "Give me ten minutes. I need to set up an encrypted link. I'll email it to you. As soon as you get it, open the link, attach the photo, and hit send. Count to twenty, then turn whatever device you're using to send the email completely off. Wait a minimum of five minutes, then restart your device."

"Okay," Hank said.

"Follow my directions exactly like I said. Give me an hour or two to play around with the photo and see if I can clear it up."

"How much is this gonna cost?" Hank asked.

"I'll only charge you if I can get a quality photo. The price will depend on how long it takes me to clear it up. Look for my link in ten minutes."

The line went dead.

"If we can get something to identify that truck, we might be able to figure out who owns it or rented it."

"The thieves were fast," Hank said. "They used the shop's engine hoist to move engines from boats to the vehicle they hauled everything away with—possibly that red truck. Mr. Phil said they'd need something that was heavy-duty since boat engines weigh so much."

"Since they didn't return the engine hoist to the shop and they just left Emmitt's truck and our boat trailer at the ramp, I bet they ran out of time."

"Maybe that's when the dog bit one of the burglars," Hank said. "If so, there could be blood in Emmitt's truck, on your trailer, or even on the pier."

"How long will it take Corker to get DNA tests back from that fur?" I asked.

"If he sends it off first thing tomorrow morning, he might have results back next week. I doubt they'll put a rush on it. Murders and rapes take precedence over robberies."

I scanned my notes. "We've got the DNA from the dog fur. Hacktivist is working on the photo of the red truck. Hopefully, Katelyn's dad can tell us if he's seen any smokers at the boat-yard. What else?"

"I did some more research on those South Carolina marina thefts. With the July marina robbery in Charleston, the cops arrived quickly. They came in a helicopter and used thermal imagery to track the thieves. They picked up heat signatures from at least six different people."

"Did they catch them on security cameras?" I asked.

"In all of those robberies, the first thing the thieves did was disable or destroy the cameras. The burglars never stepped into the field of the cameras, even when they were destroying them. You have to assume the thieves staked out each marina before-hand, so they knew the camera locations."

"If these are the same thieves," I said, "why didn't they destroy Fripp's cameras?"

"Maybe it's not the same group. After all, our thieves didn't just steal electronics, they stole engines and your boat, too. The engines would take longer to steal than just electronics."

Next, we watched the video and pictures that the police had taken of the shop and dry stacks the morning after the robbery.

You could hear Officer Cantrell narrating the video, which showed the location of the dry stacks within the rest of the boatyard. Then he walked to the marina behind the store. An eight-foot-tall chain link fence and gate separated the marina boat slips and dock from the rest of the property.

"Go back a little bit to where he was filming the dry stacks so we can see which ones don't have engines," Hank said.

"Here. Cantrell took close-up still shots of the boats," I said.

We studied the photos carefully. Fourteen of the fifteen boats on the first row had no engines. One photo showed a boat that still had its engine, but was missing some, but not all, of its electronics.

"Hey, I know that boat," I said, pointing at the lime green boat on the screen. "I saw it on Monday afternoon when we went to see our boat. They were moving it with the forklift."

"I wonder if it belongs to Mrs. Ozmore's friend. See how it still has its navigation system and fish finder, but the stereo is gone?" He pointed at the screen. "She said her friend's boat had a really nice stereo system in it."

"Her boat could be any of the boats with missing stereos."

"Go back and look at each of the close-ups again," Hank commanded.

Can't you just tell me? "I get so sick of you making me find things that you already found!"

"You said you want to be treated as an equal. Where's all your female equality rhetoric now?"

I hissed at him then pointed at the screen. "That one is missing electronics."

"*All* the other boats on the bottom row are missing *all* their electronics," Hank said, "except for the green boat." He leaned closer to the screen. "It looks like GPSea is the brand of the navigation system."

Hank searched with his phone and read silently for a few

seconds. "Okay, looks like GPSea is an inexpensive and short-range navigation system. You buy regional software packages that you download onto the system. It's good for people who never plan to use their boat outside a certain geographical area."

"*So*, if international boat thieves wanted to sell it to someone in the Caribbean, it would be useless!"

"If it didn't have the Caribbean software? Yes."

He took out his phone and scrolled through some pictures. "Hmm." He handed the phone to me and said, "This is a photo I took of the stacks on Tuesday afternoon. Notice anything?"

I scanned between the still shots Officer Cantrell had taken of the boats on the bottom row, and the ones Hank took on Tuesday afternoon that we'd loaded on my laptop.

I gasped. "Oh, I see! The green boat, the one we think is the Garfield's, was on the bottom row in slip A-1 when the cops photographed the dry stacks on Tuesday morning, but by the time we got there in the afternoon it was gone.

"On Monday when you saw them lowering the green boat, where did they take it from?"

"One of the higher rows, but I don't know exactly which one. At that point I didn't know how the slips were numbered."

"And did they put it in the water?"

I shook my head. "They put it right there." I pointed to its location in the cop's photo.

"We need to find out if that boat *is* the Garfield's boat and what slip it's assigned to."

"I think tonight is a good time for a field trip. We need to compare Cantrell's Tuesday morning photos and my Tuesday afternoon photos to the boats' locations today."

"But it's a school night," I whined.

Hank's phone pinged.

"Saved by the bell," I said.

Hank clicked on the email link Hacktivist77 sent and did all the other steps he'd been instructed to do, which culminated with him turning his phone off.

"Now we just have to wait and see whether `Hacktivist77` can make the screenshot of the truck clearer," Hank said.

"You know," I said, "my dad was taking pictures and video of our new boat on Monday. He might have caught the boats stored in dry stack in some of his photos. Our boat was parked right near there."

"Can you get them to me?" Hank asked.

"As long as Dad hasn't deleted them," I said. "And… only on the condition that we don't take a field trip to Fripp's graveyard tonight. I'm tired!" I punctuated that statement with a gaping yawn.

"Fine," he said. "Do you want to stay to see what `Hacktivist77` texts back?"

"Did you not see my yawn?"

"Jeez, grump! Go home."

20

HANK

F raud is prevalent in the marine insurance industry. It comes in many forms: buying insurance for a boat that doesn't exist; purposely sinking or crashing a boat; catching a boat on fire; or even staging a pirate attack, as one cargo ship owner did to collect a $77 million insurance payout. For more information on fraud and scams, see Forensics 411 episode 38, "When Lying Pays."

AFTER HANNAH LEFT, I took out a few pieces of printer paper and taped them end to end. With a ruler, I made a chart four rows high—one row for each of the sets of photos we had or would have of the dry stacks. The chart was fifteen blocks wide. From left to right I labeled them A-1, A-2, A-3... all the way to A-15 to represent each of the slips on the bottom row of the dry stacks. I labeled the top row *Monday evening*, then studied the photos Hannah had just texted from her dad's phone. In the second row, I would write descriptions of each of the boats in the bottom row of the dry stacks on Tuesday morning, based on Officer Cantrell's photos. The third row of my chart would be where I listed boats that were on the bottom row of the dry stacks in the pictures I took on Tuesday afternoon. The last row of boxes would have which boats were in each of those slips as of Friday when Hannah and I could go back to the boatyard after school.

After hand-drawing my chart, I needed the computer in the den to see the details of the boats. My eyes hurt from looking on my tiny phone screen.

The den door was closed so I knocked. I didn't want to catch Mom and Corker canoodling on the couch.

No one answered.

I knocked again then cracked the door.

The den was empty.

I dashed to the kitchen window. Corker's car was still in the driveway.

I seethed.

Our house was small. A den, the kitchen, three bedrooms, and two bathrooms. There was only one other place they could be...

My heart sank. Mom's bedroom door was closed.

I clenched my fists as I mentally bounced between Hannah saying that Mom deserved to have fun and my own feelings that I didn't want my mom shacking up with... well... anyone.

Right then, they came through the back door laughing, each with a glass of wine.

"Where have you been?" I demanded.

"We strolled down to the dock to look at the stars," Mom said.

"Oh, well... I didn't know where you were!"

"Sorry," she said. "I didn't know you wanted a play-by-play."

I turned to Corker. "You'll send that dog fur off to the crime lab first thing in the morning, right?"

"Uh-huh," Corker looked nervously at Mom then set his wine glass on the counter.

"Good. I really appreciate you letting us help you with the case!"

"Steve!" Mom glared at him.

Feeling satisfied that Corker was sufficiently in trouble with my mom, I pivoted to the den, opened the email I'd sent myself with all the dry stack photos, and got to work. I filled in the top three rows of my chart, one by one, noting everything I could about the appearance of each boat in each slip in each set of photos.

Around midnight, I completed those three rows, then put the chart in the shoe box in my closet with other important things.

After studying all those photos, I knew one thing for sure: the Fripps had been playing musical chairs with their customers' boats.

21

HANNAH
FRIDAY

Procure *(v.) to obtain, especially with care or effort*

ONCE AGAIN, we found ourselves riding our god-forsaken bikes to the boatyard after school.

"In first period, Katelyn seemed kind of mad that we'd done the interviews without her," I said.

"She has band practice on Wednesdays and Thursdays, then games on Fridays. Are we supposed to stop our investigation to accommodate her extra-curricular interests?"

"No, but she felt left out."

"I texted her about whether anyone at the boatyard smokes. That's including her."

"I realize that your social-emotional wherewithal has really been tested lately, so let me spell this out for you: she wants to do stuff *with* us, not *for* us," I said. "Not everyone wants to be your errand girl."

"She has to work her way up in the ranks just like you did! It's only fair."

I shook my head. "So, she's going to be your next secretary?"

"Everyone has to earn their chops," Hank said.

"Just try to keep her in the loop, okay? Invite her along."

"Fine," Hank said. "According to her dad, none of the employees at the boatyard smoke. That's useful."

"You don't keep her in the loop because she's *useful*. You keep her in the loop because you care about her feelings!"

"Feelings. Right."

"You know, coaching you on how to be human gets exhausting!"

We turned the corner at Eugene Lund's house.

"Does Hacktivist77 think he can make the screenshot of the truck clearer?" I asked.

"Yep," Hank said. "And for just a bit more, he'll trace the license plate to its owner. What do you think about that?"

I stopped pedaling, which made him stop pedaling.

"That's the whole point of getting him to clear up the screenshot. Simply having the license plate numbers doesn't do us any good. The only reason we need the license plate number is to find out who owns or rented the truck. And since you're in some sort of Oedipal competition with Corker to solve the case first, we can't have him look up the license plate number. He doesn't even know we have photos of the truck."

"What I hear you saying is you're okay with us paying a little extra for Hacktivist77 to trace the plate for us." Hank started pedaling again.

"How much extra?" I asked, scurrying to catch up.

"An extra fifty bucks," he said. "And the beauty of our business partnership is that we can pool our resources when necessary."

"I take it that you want to pull—P-U-L-L!—some of my resources?"

"Only if you want to find out who owns the flatbed."

"If I'm going to financially back this investigation, I want my name on the business cards."

"I will take that into consideration."

I changed the subject. "Did you sign up for driver's ed yet? I can't wait to get my license. I don't even care whether I get a cool car or not. I'd rather drive a station wagon than ride this stupid bike!"

"Your parents are going to buy you a car when you get your license?"

"Uh-huh."

"Must be nice!"

"If they get me a car, it helps them out. They won't have to drive me around anymore, and I can help them get Josey to soccer practice and stuff like that."

"Have they *told you* they're going to get you a car?"

"Well… no, but why wouldn't they?"

"Because cars cost a lot of money!"

"It's not like they're going to buy me a brand-new car. They'll get me something used."

Hank guffawed. "A used car? How humiliating!"

"I'm not spoiled, if that's what you're insinuating!"

"Of course not! Everybody's parents buy them a car when they get their license!" He pointed. "Let's stow our bikes behind those bushes on the far side of the boat ramp."

"Don't you think your mom will get you a car?"

"Hannah, have you noticed that we're not exactly rich?"

We hid our bikes and watched the boatyard from under a large oak tree twenty yards from Emmitt's truck.

"We're not rich!" I said defensively.

"Your dad had a two-hundred-thousand-dollar boat built for himself."

I did a double take. "Our boat cost that much?"

He scoffed. "Easily. It had two 300-horsepower Kamaha engines on it. Those alone are forty grand each!"

"Wow! I had no idea."

"Now you know," he said. "You're rich."

I considered that. "Well, when I get a car, I'll drive you to school."

"Thanks, but I don't know if I can stand the stigma of riding to school in a used station wagon." He reached in his bookbag and pulled out a flashlight.

"Don't you think it's a little bit daytime-y to need a flashlight?" I asked.

"This is ultraviolet. If Hugo bit one of the thieves hard enough to draw blood, they might've left a droplet at the scene."

"What if Emmitt washed his truck after the robbery?" I asked.

"Then we need to get inside the truck and see if there's any blood there," he said. "Come on." Hank grabbed my hand and pulled me to Emmitt's truck.

He inspected the truck by shining the ultraviolet flashlight on the vehicle body. Then he took a picture of the license plate. Next, he peeked in all the windows.

"This truck has a push-button start."

"My mom's minivan has that, too. I don't get the appeal. I mean how taxing could it be to turn a key? The push button start doesn't save time and you still have to have your keys with you to start the car, so it's not like it helps you when you can't find your keys."

"A push-button start system can't be hot-wired," Hank said.

"Then how did the thieves start Emmitt's truck?"

Hank crouched down and checked under the body of the truck. "I'm looking for one of those hide-a-key containers. It's a little box you can stick an extra key in and hide it under the body of your vehicle with a magnet."

"I'm familiar with the concept."

"Voices!"

We darted behind the shrubs and watched.

Emmitt and Brock were walking toward his truck.

"… date at ten when she gets off of work," Emmitt said.

"Am I ever going to get to meet this mystery girl?" Brock asked.

"We're taking it slow," Emmitt said.

"Are you *sure* she's not married?"

"Don't worry about it," Emmitt said. "I know what I'm doing."

The brothers got in and drove away.

"He used his key fob to unlock the door," Hank said. "Keyless locks can't be picked. You have to use a transponder programming tool to get keyless cars unlocked."

"And for that matter, why did the truck start for the thieves when it wouldn't start for Emmitt?" I said.

"Let's assume the thieves had a transponder programmer with them. They would've also needed a spare key fob they could program to open, then start the truck."

"But once they got in the car and tried to start it, they realized something was wrong," I said. "The truck wouldn't start."

"Right. So, our thieves took the time and had the skill to fix the mechanical issue when Emmitt couldn't even figure out what was wrong. *Then,* they drove it over to the gravel area, hitched up your boat, backed it down the ramp, and drove the boat away, leaving the truck and trailer at the ramp."

"That seems like it would take an awful lot of time." I tucked a piece of wayward hair back into my ponytail. "Maybe the truck was unlocked. That would've saved the thieves a couple minutes of breaking-in time."

"They'd still have to program their spare key fob to *start* the truck," Hank said. "After they attempted to start it, they'd realize something was wrong with the truck, and have to either give up or diagnose *and fix* the truck. Unless..."

He gaped at me as if I were supposed to finish his sentence.

"Is this another one of your 'teachable moments'?" I asked.

He nodded.

I considered why the thieves would've invested so much

time in reprogramming a key fob and fixing Emmitt's broken-down truck just to steal our boat.

He said it again. "Unless…"

I gasped. "Oh, I know!" I bounced up and down. "*Unless* the thieves didn't have to do any of that because the truck wasn't actually broken down!"

HANK

P*ost-Traumatic Stress Disorder is a mental health condition that can occur after experiencing or witnessing a terrifying event. Symptoms can include lack of concentration, anxiety, nightmares, chest pains, headaches, mutism, feelings of isolation, depression and engaging in destructive behavior. For more information, see* Forensics 411 *episode 32, "Understanding the Victim."*

AFTER WE TOOK our fourth set of photos of the dry stacks, Hannah said the words I never wanted to hear on a Friday evening: "Let's go to McDiggle's."

It was the last place I wanted to be before the first football game of the year, but I couldn't think of a good excuse to avoid it.

We leaned our bikes against the dumpster in the back of the parking lot. I hung back a bit and let Hannah go in first, hoping the crowd size would squelch her craving for a burger.

The restaurant was crammed with kids from school.

As she opened the door, loud, excited conversations assaulted my ears.

"Whoa, this place is packed!"

"Uh-huh," I murmured.

Hannah surveyed the crowd. "It seems like the whole school is here!"

"Yep." I slid back out the doorway.

"Come on," Hannah said. "I wonder if Katelyn's here."

My heart was racing, and I felt sweat bead on the back of my neck and forehead. "She's in the band. They have to be at the school early for the game."

"It looks like everyone is here."

You said that.

I dropped back against the side of the building.

"Hank? What's wrong?"

"I... um... I can't go in there."

"How come?"

I felt myself slipping down the tunnel.

"Dillon and the Madisons will be in there. This is their turf," I said. "Everyone comes here before home football games."

"There's a football game tonight?"

"Don't you listen to the morning announcements?"

"I have Miss Kessler for homeroom. I think this is her first teaching job, and she can't control us. It's too loud to hear anything in that room."

She squatted beside me, took my hand, and massaged it between the thumb and pointer finger as she'd done in the hallway on the first day of school. "You've just got to learn how to control it. Otherwise, Dillon wins," she said. "This is only their turf if you let it be."

What she said was reminiscent of Dr. Blanchard's advice to "write my own narrative."

"We could go to the House of Pizza," I said, starting to feel myself coming out of the tunnel of panic.

Hannah stared at the police station across the street.

"Let's go to the game! One of my parents could drive us."

And there I went—careening back down the tunnel. My heart pounded and I began to hyperventilate.

I ripped my hand out of Hannah's and bolted toward my bike. "I'm sorry. I can't!"

"Wait! Don't leave!"

"I can't go in there!" I yelled as I pedaled out of the parking lot.

"Stop!" Hannah shouted. "At least wait for me!"

I kept pedaling. "Just go in if that's what you want! Break bread with the Madisons!"

I FRANTICALLY BIKED HOME.

A few minutes later Hannah was calling from the kitchen. "I know you're here," she said. "Please talk to me. I want to help."

"What's all the racket?" Grandpa called from the den.

"Sorry, Mr. Boyd. It's me, Hannah. I just needed to talk to Hank. I should've knocked."

"You should've knocked!" he parroted.

"I'm really sorry. I just need to speak with Hank."

Hannah tapped on my bedroom door.

"Go away!"

"No."

"Yes."

"No," she said. "I'm not going away because if I do this will turn into another fight, and we agreed we weren't going to do that anymore."

She cracked the door open and peeked through. "Can I come in?"

"Whatever."

"I let myself in the house."

"Obviously."

She sank down on the bed next to me. "Are you feeling any better?"

"I'm no longer in panic mode, if that's what you mean."

"Good."

We both stared silently at my *X-Files* poster for an uncomfortable minute.

"Um, what happened back there?" she asked.

"I don't go to football games."

"Any particular reason why?"

"Yes."

"Are you going to tell me?"

"No."

"Any particular reason why?"

"Yes."

"And... what might that be?" She touched my shoulder. "Please, you can tell me. You know my darkest secret so—"

"So, I'm just supposed to tell you mine, then we're even-steven?"

"Not *even-steven*. It's just that I shared something really personal with you about having to go to that hospital, and I want you to feel that you can do the same."

I repositioned myself to face her. "If I tell you, you can't ever tell anyone else—not your parents, not Josey, not Katelyn. There are only a few people who know what happened. And we don't even know what *really* happened."

"Who's we?" she asked.

"Me, my mom, Grandpa and—I think—Miss Danielle, Katelyn's mom. I'm fairly sure my mom told her about it."

"What?"

"What happened to me in sixth grade."

"Okay. What happened?"

I took a deep breath. "You can't tell anyone!"

"I won't."

"The story my mom told the principal and my teachers was that I got hit by a car."

Hannah gasped, and her hand flew to her mouth.

"The public library is across the parking lot from the middle school. I used to go there after school on Tuesdays, then my mom would pick me up after work. On the first day of sixth grade, I met a kid named Jackson. He said he was on the other sixth grade team, so we didn't have any classes together. He said he had first lunch and I had second. We seemed to hit it off. I mean, he was reading a book about forensics when I first met him." I swallowed hard. "He invited me to go to the middle school football game that Thursday after school. I bought my ticket. He told me to wait for him behind the concession stand if I got there first. The last thing I remember is looking at my watch. Three days later I woke up in the hospital."

Hannah gasped again.

"Mom went to pick me up after the game, but she couldn't find me. I didn't have a cell phone back then. She drove all around the school, the high school, the park, the library, House of Pizza, McDiggle's, any place she could think of. After about an hour, she called the police. Since Chief Buckley is an idiot, he told her I had to be missing twenty-four hours before she could file a missing person report." I shook my head. "That's a myth perpetuated by inaccurate cop shows."

"What about Jackson? What happened to him?"

"No one knows," I said. "Mom and Grandpa drove around town for hours looking for me or anyone who'd seen me. It was only the third day of school; most people didn't even know who I was. They eventually found me in a ditch near The Compound."

"Holy crap!"

"I don't remember any of that, but Mom's told me that Grandpa was the one who actually found me. She said I was cut, bruised, in shock, and just conscious enough to moan."

"Oh my gosh!"

My left arm and three ribs were broken." I got a lump in my throat.

Hannah leaned over and hugged me. "I'm truly sorry that happened to you."

I whispered "thanks" into her hair, then pulled away.

"I couldn't talk for about two weeks after it happened. They ran all kinds of tests to find out if I had damage to the part of my brain that controls speech. I didn't. My doctor at the hospital recommended Dr. Blanchard. He came while I was still in the hospital and said I had Post-Traumatic Stress Disorder. The reason I couldn't remember what happened that night was because my brain was trying to protect itself from the knowledge of the event. Dr. B said I had anxiety-induced mutism associated with my PTSD, and that it would eventually correct itself. Which it did."

Hannah held her hands in front of her as if praying.

"Wow. You had an actual childhood trauma. I'm so sorry for joking about that," she said. "*Did* you get hit by a car?"

I shrugged. "It's a better explanation than to think that a guy who I thought was my friend beat me up and left me in a ditch."

"Did they look for Jackson? What was his last name?"

"I never asked him his last name. That was stupid of me. I described him to the cops, but he just looked like a regular sixth grade kid. The principal gave the cops and me copies of the middle school yearbooks from the previous few years, and yearbooks from all the elementary schools that feed into Vista Point Middle. There were six kids named Jackson in those yearbooks, but none of them were the one I knew. It's like he dropped off the face of the earth," I said. "The doctor thought my injuries were consistent with having been hit by a car, so that's what my mom told everybody at school." My hand shook slightly. "Dr. B thought it might be best to do homebound instruction for a bit. I would've been happy to do homeschool forever, but eventually, Dr. Blanchard said it was important for my 'healing process' to go back to school. I returned second semester of sixth grade, but everyone had made friends and had their groups so…"

A tear rolled down her cheek. "Oh, my god, that's what happened to me when I went back to school after Ben died."

"I recognized the similarities between our stories when your mom told me."

"That's why you didn't want to go to the football game?" She sniffled.

"Yes."

"And you have no idea what really happened to you or who did it?"

"The cops never found 'Jackson,' but I've always thought that Dillon Buckley had something to do with it."

"Dillon? You think he hates you *that* much and has the ability to orchestrate something like that?" Hannah asked. "Just because you hit him with a boomerang back in first grade?"

"Oh, there've been lots of other things over the years," I said, not wanting to recount the teasing; the harassment; the pantsing incidents; the number of times he'd rolled my yard with toilet paper; all the times he stole my homework and put his name on it; how he tripped me in the hall just the other day; how he attacked me at the police station over the summer.

"He's evil," I said. "And that's not hyperbole. In fifth grade, our teacher, Mr. Wallace, caught him cheating on a big test and gave him a zero for it. That zero added to all his other pathetic grades made Dillon fail math for the whole year. He had to go to summer school. To get back at our teacher, Dillon went to the principal and told him that Mr. Wallace had forced him to look at a magazine with naked women in it. Mr. Wallace denied it, and I'm sure it wasn't true. He was one of the best teachers I've ever had. Dillon told the principal that Mr. Wallace kept the dirty magazines in his classroom filing cabinet. The principal searched the classroom and found them right where Dillon said they'd be. Mr. Wallace got fired.

"That's horrible."

"Of course, Dillon couldn't keep his mouth shut. Over the summer he bragged to some kids that the magazines belonged to his brother and that he put them in the filing cabinet one day while everyone was at recess. He said he'd wanted to teach Mr. Wallace a lesson about messing with him."

"Over-confidence always gets you!"

"I know. So, I told my mom, who called the principal. I don't know what sort of investigation the principal did, but Mr. Wallace ended up being transferred to another school rather than being fired entirely."

"Did Dillon know that your mom was the one that told the principal?"

"I certainly never took credit for it. But Dillon Buckley believes what he wants to believe."

"Do you think Dillon somehow staged your meeting Jackson and then beat you up or had Jackson beat you up? Or that he had someone hit you with a car? That's quite a plot for a kid to come up with on his own. Besides, what kind of kid *does* that?"

"The kind of kid who would plant porno magazines in his teacher's filing cabinet because the teacher gave him the F that he deserved!"

Hannah pulled her knees up against her chest. "Jeez, I can't believe that. It's beyond awful."

I took a deep breath and revealed something I'd never said out loud. "It makes it hard to trust people."

"No kidding!" Hannah shifted toward me and looked me squarely in the eyes. "This explains so much." She patted my knee. "I promise I'll never hurt you like that. Never."

"I don't think I'll ever be able to go to a football game again. And I just didn't want to go into McDiggle's tonight because of all the people that were in there. I avoid Dillon whenever I can. It's not because I'm afraid of him; I just don't like him," I said. "I'm sorry I freaked out, but I appreciate your help—you know, rubbing my hand and stuff... and the fact that you came here after me."

"You're welcome," she said bumping her shoulder against mine.

23

HANNAH

I **niquitous** *(adj.) grossly unfair and morally wrong*

WHEN I GOT home from Hank's, I went straight upstairs, jumped in the shower, and cried. Our stories, the bad parts at least, were incredibly similar. When we were eleven years old, fate, horrible people, or *both* dealt us an unwinnable hand of cards. It was more than I'd been able to handle.

He'd lost a father he never even had. I'd lost Ben. We'd both been robbed of something. Our childhoods? Our middle school years? Our innocence? Maybe even our ability to trust.

Who expects an old woman to be driving drunk at three o'clock in the afternoon, run up on a curb, and hit a group of third graders?

Probably the same ones who would beat up a kid (*or hit them with a car*) and leave them for dead in a ditch.

I dried off from my shower but continued to cry for Ben, Hank, myself and all the tragedy in the world. Sometimes it overwhelmed me.

Most of the time it overwhelmed me.

24

HANK

Beginning in the mid-1990s, police departments installed an increasing number of cameras in public spaces like housing projects, schools and parks. Closed-circuit television (CCTV) later became common in banks and stores to discourage theft. Most security camera footage is stored for 30 to 90 days, but banks are required to keep theirs for up to six months. See Forensics 411 *episode 43, "Everyone Say 'Cheese,'" for more information about security cameras.*

AFTER HANNAH LEFT, I received a text from `Hacktivist77`: `Truck part of rental fleet. No writing on cab. License plate is Indiana SP929DCB. Trailer and cargo carrier rented 8/31 from Coastal Freight Logistics in Wilmington, NC by Roy Buck Denley. Paid cash for one-way rental to Florida.`

25

HANNAH

SATURDAY MORNING

Internet (n.) an interconnected network of computers using standardized communication protocols whose original concept was first developed in 1962

"LET ME GET THIS STRAIGHT," I said as we walked. "We can go to McDiggle's for breakfast but not dinner on a Friday night?"

"Seriously?" Hank said, "You're going to harass me?"

"I'm sorry," I said. "You won't let me tease you about your hairy father's terrorist roots so can't I at least rag on you about your McIssues?"

"No."

We ordered some biscuits and sodas and claimed a corner booth.

"Let's talk about your daddy issues."

"I no longer have those."

"Puhleaze, everyone has daddy issues."

"I know his name. I know he wasn't a sleezeball *or* a terrorist. My mom loved him... I'm good."

"I don't believe you. Letting a sleeping dog lie is not your forte. Aren't you curious to find anything else out?"

He shrugged. "I'd like to know more, but I don't know how to find more information. The other night I checked online, and only about twenty percent of Afghans have internet access. In fact, only a third of the country has electricity twenty-four hours a day."

"Sounds like there's a twenty percent chance your Afghan relatives are on Instagram."

"I doubt it. But it would be pretty dope if I had aunts, uncles, and cousins! I'm an only child and my mom is too, so I've never had any extended family."

I set my biscuit down and said, "There is something incongruous about your utterance of the word *dope*. Let's not *ever* use that word again."

"Oh, sorry."

"Forgiven," I said. "Your mom said your dad had a sister, right?"

"Yes, and she must've been older if they left Afghanistan right after Dad was born."

"Aww! You just called him 'Dad,'" I said. "You *like* him, like him!"

"I like knowing his story. I wish I knew more about him and his family."

"Have you heard of this new thing called the internet? Apparently even twenty percent of Afghanistan has it!" I said. "Maybe you could find them through *MyDNAHistory.com*. Don't they have family trees and that sort of thing on their website?"

"Yes, but only if my broadly Central Asian family members also happened to have their DNA tested through the same company. That's a longshot. The reason *MyDNAHistory* couldn't be more specific than to tell me I'm 'broadly Central Asian' is because they don't have a good sample size from that part of the world. The countries are rural. The people are poor, and Afghanistan's been at war off and on for centuries. I doubt that getting a hundred-dollar DNA test is high on anyone's priorities. They're just trying to survive."

"What about online newspapers? If your paternal grandfather was in the government back then, maybe he still is."

"That was more than forty years ago. I'm gonna guess he's retired or dead by now."

"Maybe you could find your father's obituary online."

He shook his head while he chewed his biscuit. "I already checked. No obituary."

"Once we solve this burglary, we can jump full force into learning more about the Khalud family," I said.

26

HANK

O nly limited genetic information can be obtained from saliva using typical serum tests. However, scientists have had success using a special kind of test to create DNA profiles from saliva left on smoked cigarettes. Seventy-four percent of the DNA in saliva comes from white blood cells, which contain high quality genome material. Therefore, like blood, saliva can be reliably used for DNA analysis. See Forensics 411 episode 7, "Secrets of the Body."

WE LEFT McDiggle's and walked to the boatyard with the mission of finding cigarette butts with the DNA of one of the burglars.

"This Roy Buck Denley rented the red tractor-trailer locally," Hannah said, "so maybe it *was* locals who committed the burglary."

We made the turn at Mr. Lund's house onto Marina Lane. "Google that name and see what you get. I'll lookup Coastal Freight Logistics."

"See," Hannah said. "Walking is way better. You can't surf the net while riding a bike."

"Coastal Freight Logistics is located near the Port of Wilmington, all the way downtown," I said.

Hannah put her arms up. "There is absolutely *no way* I am riding or walking to downtown Wilmington! That's like twenty miles."

"No, we'll have to get a ride if it comes to that."

"I've got a Roy David Buck who's a first-degree arsonist in Colorado," Hannah said looking at her phone. "Then there's a Roy Buck Dean who ran for mayor of Fayetteville, Arkansas back in 1984. He lost." She continued reading. "An artist named Roy Donley paints Alaskan landscapes. There's also the famous Ray Burk Dennelly, a firefighter in El Paso, Texas. And of course, there's the notorious Sears Roebuck."

"Roy Buck Denley might've used a fake name," I said.

The marina, boatyard and boat ramp were chaotic. The parking lot for boat trailers, located behind Leslie Davis's house, was packed. It was the Saturday of Labor Day weekend, the unofficial end of summer. The mayhem would make it easier to sneak into the fenced area unnoticed and look for cigarette butts.

"Did you invite Katelyn to do this with us?" Hannah asked.

"Actually, because I'm trying to be one of those friend-thingies, I did. She said she was going to the mall."

"The mall on such a pretty day?"

"Why anyone would *ever* want to go to the mall is beyond me," I said. "It's the tenth circle of hell that Dante never could have predicted." I took two zipper bags and two pairs of latex gloves out of my backpack. "Here, don't touch any of the cigarettes directly. We need to preserve the existing DNA."

"It hasn't gone unnoticed that you no longer carry your boomerang tucked in the back of your pants," Hannah said. "Is that so you can bring your backpack full of CSI goodies instead?"

"Exactly," I answered. "Let's use a quadrant search pattern. Do you remember how to do that?"

"Remember?" Hannah teased. "I watch episode sixteen of

Forensics 411 every night before I go to bed. It's like taking a prescription strength sleeping pill."

"You start in quadrant one by the store and move to two. I'll start in quadrant three by the mechanic's shop and move to four. Be fast."

We scampered across the gravel parking lot looking for cigarette butts. Less than five minutes later, we met in the middle. Hannah had two cigarette butts. I had three.

"Five total," Hannah said. "The surgeon general and American Lung Association have done their job well."

"Yeah," I said.

"Hey! You two. What are you doing?" Brock Fripp yelled at us.

Hannah and I stuffed the plastic bags and latex gloves in my backpack.

"I'll handle this," I said.

Brock traipsed over to us. "You see that forklift? It's carrying a ten-thousand-pound boat. You want that to fall on you?"

"Oh, sorry," I said. "We're looking for my dog. He got out, and we thought he might've come over here. I just live down the road." I pointed to Leslie Davis's house.

"What's the dog look like?"

Hannah must've picked up on my plan because she said, "He's a white German Shepard named Hugo. You know, he's got pointy ears, about this tall." She made a motion with her hands.

The forklift engine cut off.

"What're you kids doing back here?" Emmitt fumed while bolting across the gravel. He appeared unnecessarily angry.

"They're lookin' for their dog," Brock said. "It's that white one that lives over yonder in the house near the boat ramp."

Emmitt's eyes narrowed. "You live over there? That white dog's yours?"

I nodded.

"You need to keep that thing locked up. It bit somebody the other night!"

"Really? Who?"

"Just someone using the boat ramp."

"*At night?*" Hannah asked.

"No!—day—he bit someone the other day!" Emmitt said.

"Did you see it happen?" I asked. "Did he have to go to the doctor? If you know the person's name, I can have my mom call him and offer to pay his medical bills."

"I don't know his name!" Emmitt groused. "But his hand was bleeding good."

"It was his hand?" Hannah said.

Emmitt seemed frustrated. "Listen, just get out of here and don't come back. This area is restricted. And keep that dog of yours locked up!"

Brock turned to us. "I didn't hear about anybody getting bit, but if the guy that got bit wanted to, he could call animal control. They'll take that dog of yours away."

"Well, we better go find him, then," I said.

When we were through the fence, Hannah whispered, "Did you catch that he said the person was bitten at *night*?"

"The boat ramp closes at dusk," I said. "And he knew Hugo bit the person *on the hand*. What do you think the chances are that Hugo bit someone *other* than one of the burglars when he escaped from his yard the night of the burglary?"

"Not good."

27

HANNAH

C ***ryptic*** *(adj.) having a meaning that is mysterious, puzzling, enigmatic*

WE SAT on the floor of Hank's bedroom. His puke-green carpet had become our war room when working a case.

"We had a productive day," I said. "We confirmed that Hugo bit someone. And, either Emmitt *saw* him bite the person, or someone with knowledge of the incident told him about it."

"Did you notice how he got nervous when I asked him for details?" Hank asked.

"And did you catch that Brock hadn't heard anything about a dog bite?"

"Seems like it would've been news, at least in the Fripp family, if someone were bitten by a dog on their property. Most people are afraid of being sued."

"And since Emmitt knows where Hugo lives, you'd think he would have told the victim."

I studied Hank's dark paneled walls. The Boyds had clearly never attempted to bring their 1970s house into this millennium.

"How likely do you think it is that the thieves had a key fob, a transponder, and a knowledge of mechanical issues that allowed them to start and use Emmitt's truck in the robbery?" I asked. "I mean... seriously."

Hank tapped our case notebook. "Let's list Emmitt as a person of interest."

"Do you think he worked with the thieves?"

"It's *possible*," Hank said. "But possible and probable are two different things. If we decide it's a real theory to present to Corker, we've got to have solid evidence. Nobody is going to readily believe that the son robbed his own father. It makes no sense, especially considering how much the burglary has hurt Mr. Fripp's business."

"What about Roy Buck Denley?" I skimmed our notes. "He rented the flatbed and cargo container in Wilmington. He might have even driven it to and from the burglary."

"Hacktivist77 said that Roy Buck Denley rented the truck *one-way*... to Florida." Hank swept the hair from his forehead. "Florida's closer to the Caribbean than North Carolina."

"Who's got mad geography skills?" I playfully punched him in the arm.

"I'm just saying that it would make sense to take everything they stole down to Florida because that's one step closer to getting it the Caribbean."

"Did you ask Corker to put out an APB for the truck and Roy Buck Denley?"

"I haven't given him the license plate or name yet."

"Why not?"

"Because I want to solve this case without him," Hank said.

"This rivalry between you and Corker is getting old," I said. "Why not just challenge him to an arm-wrestling contest to see which one of you gets your mom."

"It's not like that," Hank insisted.

"Sure seems like it." I curled my lip. "Whether you like it or not, we need Steve. No one's going to pay attention to an APB issued by *us*."

Hank moseyed to his closet and came back with a long paper.

"This is the chart I've been making." He explained how he organized the rows to correspond with the four sets of photos we had of the dry stacks from Monday evening, Tuesday morning, Tuesday afternoon, and Friday.

"We need to go through the pictures from Friday and complete the last row of the chart."

I leaned over his shoulder as he wrote. After three seconds of me inside his personal bubble, he said, "Let's make you your own copy."

He went to the den and came back with a set of papers for me.

"Here," he handed me a roll of tape.

"Jeez, you have horrible handwriting," I said. "What's this first column say."

"That's slip A-1." Hank read. "On Monday evening before the robbery they put Lacy Garfield's bright green Sea Craft-22 there. That same boat is in slip A-1 in Officer Cantrell's photos from Tuesday morning, but it no longer has a stereo system. The thieves didn't take the Johnston engine or any other electronics."

"You said thieves prefer Kamaha engines, right?"

Hank nodded. "By Tuesday afternoon the bright green boat was moved to slip D-12, and was still there Friday," Hank said. "In the two most recent photos slip A-1 has been empty."

"Okay, let me see if I can decipher your cuneiform," I said. "On Monday when my dad took his photos, a blue boat named *Reel Fun* was in A-2." I inspected Cantrell's photos on my laptop. "Tuesday morning there's a beige Whaler in slip A-2. It has no engines, and it looks like all of its electronics are gone."

"The Whaler was still in A-2 on Tuesday afternoon," Hank said. "But by Friday, *Reel Fun* was back. It's Johnston engines and electronics appear to be intact."

"So, *Reel Fun* must've been moved from slip A-2 *after* my dad took his pictures on Monday but *before* the robbery."

"Maybe the owners came to get *Reel Fun* after you were at the boatyard on Monday, took it out for some *real fun,* and didn't bring it back for a few days."

"Ooh, you're so punny!" I said.

"That would mean that Emmitt and Brock temporarily put the Whaler in *Reel Fun's* empty spot," Hank said.

"I thought each boat was assigned a specific slip on the dry stacks so when owners called to have their boat put in the water Emmitt and Brock would easily find the right boat."

"That's how most marinas operate," Hank said. "But Old Man Fripp doesn't seem very organized. Plus, Mr. Phil said that Fripp has only rented half the slips."

"And I guess if he assigns a lighter boat to the bottom row and then a heavier boat comes along, he'd have to move the lighter boat up on the stacks. That could explain why boats are getting moved around so much. He has to keep adjusting the boat positions as he rents out new slips."

I clucked my tongue and groaned.

"What?"

"There is *another* explanation for the boat movement. It means we're wasting our time, and I'm doing unnecessary damage to my eyes trying to interpret your handwriting."

"What's that?" Hank asked.

"Maybe as customers found out that boats on the bottom row were burglarized, they requested that theirs be moved to a higher level. They'd be more secure up high as long as the burglars weren't acrobats."

"Hmm." Hank scratched his head. "That would explain the movement of boats *after* the robbery, but not *before.* And you can't just move a much heavier boat to a higher level on the dry stacks. The structure wouldn't be stable," Hank said.

We continued to fill in boxes, looking for some kind of pattern.

"In my dad's photos from Monday there was a boat called *Gettin' Jiggy* in A-3. But Tuesday a boat called *Gritty Britches* was in that spot. No engines. No electronics. The thieves took everything."

"*Gritty Britches* was there on Tuesday afternoon, but by Friday *Gettin' Jiggy* was back in slip A-3. Does *Gettin' Jiggy* have Kamaha engines?"

I examined the chart. "Nope, but the boat in A-4 does... well... it *did*." I studied our photos from Friday. "Interesting."

"What?"

"The blue Sea Scout in A-4 never moved. It's in the same position in all four sets of photos."

Looking at the chart, Hank said, "They took the Kamaha engines and the multifunction display system from the boat in A-4, but not the stereo system."

I zoomed in on Hank's photos from Tuesday afternoon and turned the screen so he could see it. "It has a Scanasonic stereo. That's the brand with the anti-theft tracking device, right?"

"I'll give them one thing," Hank said. "Our thieves aren't dumb."

"A-5," Hank said. "Monday afternoon we've got a boat called *Just Chillin'* with one 400-horsepower Kamaha engine. On Tuesday morning, *Just Chillin'* was still there, but it no longer had its engine or any of its electronics."

"Tuesday afternoon, same thing: *Just Chillin'* in A-5," I said. "But on Friday, a boat called *Black Betty* is in A-5. Nothing was taken from it."

"Go to the pictures I took yesterday," Hank said. "There should be some that show the entire dry stack structure."

Chaucer wandered in as I opened the email.

"Hey there, Cutie!" I said. "What are you up to on this lovely Saturday afternoon? Something more fun than what we're doing?"

Chaucer lay down next to me on the floor, put his head in my lap, and yawned.

"Not so much, huh?" I ran a hand along his velvety ears.

"There!" Hank said, pointing at the screen. "On Friday, *Just Chillin'* is in C-6."

"This is giving me a headache. I need some water."

Hank studied the photos.

"Hello! Can you get your guest a cold beverage?"

"I'm not your waiter," Hank said.

"I'm not your secretary!" I retorted.

"Fine!" He jumped up and came back with a glass of ice water.

Chaucer sighed.

After taking a few gulps, I said, "We know that all the boats on the bottom row had things stolen from them."

"Yes."

"*Just Chillin'* was on the bottom row in A-5 on Monday and Tuesday, got burglarized, and has been moved to C-6 and a boat called *Black Betty* is now in A-5," I said. "Where was *Black Betty* on Monday and Tuesday?"

Hank checked the photo that showed the entire dry stack structure. "B-11."

"*Black Betty*'s owner was lucky their boat wasn't in A-5 the night of the robbery," I said. "The bright green boat I saw being moved from a higher row to slip A-1 on Monday had its stereo system taken that night. Those owners, the Garfields, were *unlucky.*"

I stood up and moved to the window. "Maybe we've got this all wrong. We *think* the boats on the bottom row of the dry stacks got robbed because the bottom row is the easiest for the thieves to get to—right?"

Hank agreed.

"But what if the boats on the bottom row were placed there *specifically because* the bottom row is the easiest for the thieves to get to?"

Hank rubbed his temples.

He nodded slowly. "You're saying that the Fripps might have

moved the green boat to slip A-1 before the robbery intentionally —because it had a nice stereo?"

"Exactly! The thieves only took the stereo off that boat, not the Johnston engines and not any of the other electronics. Katelyn's dad said the thieves liked the good stuff. "

I turned to him. "Think about it. The blue Sea Scout in slip A-4 never moved. The two 300-horsepower Kamaha engines, and all electronics except for the Scanasonic stereo were taken."

Hank scanned the chart. "*Just Chillin'* that was in A-5 for the robbery is only sixteen-feet-long and has one engine."

"One *Kamaha* engine," I said.

"*Black Betty*'s twenty-four feet long with two Johnston engines. She'd be a lot heavier than *Just Chillin'*. It doesn't make sense for *Just Chillin'* to be on the bottom level of the dry stacks."

I recognized the look in his eyes. "You think I'm right!" I threw my arms into the air as if I'd just stuck a perfect landing in a gymnastics competition. "The Fripps might have been re-arranging the boats so the ones with the most desirable engines and electronics were on the bottom row of the stacks—"

"Ahead of the burglary," Hank said with uncharacteristic solemnity. "You know what it means?"

I let myself fall onto his bed and exhaled. "It was an inside job."

28

HANK

C ircumstantial evidence relies on an inference to connect the evidence to a conclusion of fact. For instance, finding a person's fingerprints at a robbery crime scene does not necessarily mean that person robbed the business. That person's fingerprints could be at the crime scene due to other circumstances, such as having recently shopped at the business or being an employee. See Forensics 411 *episode 3, "Understanding Evidence."*

"You hungry?" Hannah asked.

I could tell by the look in her eyes that it was a rhetorical question. *She* was the one who was hungry.

"My mom's at the store right now, but I can probably find you something to eat."

Chaucer followed us into the kitchen as Mom came in the back door with groceries and Steve in tow.

"Oh, hi, Hannah," Ms. Boyd said. "I didn't know you were coming over."

"We're working on a school project," I said.

Mom peered past us to the papers on the floor of my bedroom.

"Why don't you two work out here in the kitchen? There's no reason to sit on your bedroom floor when we have a perfectly good table out here."

"We have more privacy in my room," I said.

"I need to be going anyway." Hannah turned to me. "We can finish analyzing the last row of data individually. I think we're onto something." Grabbing her laptop and backpack from the bedroom she waved and said, "I guess I'll see you tomorrow. Bye."

While Mom put food in the refrigerator, I lured Corker over to the pantry and whispered, "Have you been back to the boatyard?"

"Yes. I found out the stuff stolen from the shop was worth eighty-seven thousand dollars, and that's the wholesale price. Fripp says the twenty-one stolen engines total more than half a million dollars."

"Twenty-one? That's a lot of engines to steal in a short period of time," I said. "Did you get that dog fur sent off to the crime lab?"

"Uh-huh."

"Emmitt Fripp told me that Leslie Davis's dog bit one of their customers on the hand one night this week," I said.

"Maybe Emmitt's mistaken about which dog did the biting," Corker said.

"Nope. We didn't mention the dog, or anyone being bitten. He told *us* that it was Hugo and that the victim was someone using the boat ramp one *night* this week. We questioned why someone would be using the ramp at night, and he back-pedaled, saying that the person got bitten during the day."

"What are you getting at?" Corker asked.

"*What am I getting at?*" I said a little too loudly.

Mom glanced over at us.

I lowered my voice. "The *only* time Hugo escaped from his fenced yard was the night of the robbery. The only time Hugo had blood on his fur was the morning *after* the robbery. Hugo had no visible injuries, so the blood on the fur was not his. It's not unreasonable to conclude that Hugo bit someone during his time outside the fence in the wee hours of Tuesday morning, and since Emmitt volunteered the information that Hugo bit someone at the boat ramp…"

"That's circumstantial evidence."

"But when you get the DNA results back, we'll have a name, and I bet it will be someone who has a police record and likes to take other people's things."

Corker sighed.

"Have you talked to Emmitt Fripp at all?" I asked.

"Just about his truck being used to move the Simmons's boat."

"What did he say?"

"He said it wouldn't start, so he left it there overnight and rode home with Brock."

"Did he say why Brock had driven to work that day?"

"No, why would he?"

"Because the two of them usually ride together."

"Did he ever figure out what was wrong with the truck?"

"Nope. He says the thieves fixed it for him."

"That was kind of them," I said, walking to my room.

I came back with the bag of cigarette butts. When Mom went in the bathroom, I handed them to Corker.

"These are cigarette butts we found at the crime scene. If you go back and watch the shop video, you'll see that one of the burglars was smoking. According to Phil Calhoun, none of the employees smoke. One or all of these cigarettes could have DNA from our burglars on them. Is there any chance you can send them to the crime lab for analysis, too?"

"I can't afford any more DNA testing," Corker said. "When you're an adult, you'll understand that everything costs money, and you have to make choices."

"And when you're a *real* cop, you'll understand that anything can be the evidence needed to solve a crime!"

I went in my bedroom and slammed the door behind me.

29

HANNAH

L iability *(n.) the state of being responsible for something,
especially by law*

As I WALKED HOME, Hank texted me: You didn't have to
leave.

Me: Your mom obviously doesn't want us
hanging out in your bedroom.

Hank: I don't want her eavesdropping on our
conversations about the case. She gets all
irritable about me helping Corker.

I didn't respond.

Hank: If the Fripps staged the robbery (or
know who did) the evidence has to be at the
boatyard.

I texted a thumbs up to him, then added: Do I feel
another field trip coming on?

Hank texted back: Tonight?

I grumbled, then texted: OK, but I want Sunday off!
Even God rested on the seventh day!

Hank: Meet me under the oak tree at the intersection between our houses at midnight.

Me: I am soooo over biking. Can't we take your boat?

He didn't immediately answer. If he told me I was going to have to ride my bike to that boatyard again, I was going on strike.

After about fifteen minutes he responded: Be at your dock at 12:30. Wear dark clothes/ mask.

AT A LITTLE AFTER MIDNIGHT, I tiptoed down the steps that connected mine and Josey's third floor deck to the main floor. Hearing voices, I pushed myself up against the side of the house and peeked around the corner toward the neighbor's.

Nobody was outside at the Petersons' next door, and Mom and Dad were asleep.

I skulked down the steps, sticking to the shadows as best I could. Thirty yards separated me from the gate to our dock.

As I turned the corner to the back of the house, the Petersons' dog, an annoying little mutt named Trigger, spotted me and felt the need to tell the world.

I picked up a stick and threw it as hard as I could into the Peterson's yard. When he spun to investigate, I darted across our backyard with the gate key in hand. Just as I closed the gate behind me, he ran to the side fence and let me know he'd seen me.

I hid behind the wooden door until I heard one of the Petersons call Trigger into the house.

"It's about time," I whispered.

After the barker went inside, I still heard muffled voices in the distance.

I turned three-hundred-sixty degrees, saw no one, then put my ski mask on.

"Maybe I *am* schizophrenic?" I whispered. "I hear voices, and now I'm talking to myself."

With a new moon the stars really twinkled. Hank paddled out from behind some vegetation that grew along the waterway.

I scurried toward his boat, climbed aboard, and whispered, "Do you hear voices?"

"I think it's campers over on one of the marsh islands. Without wind, noise travels more easily over the water. Grab an oar."

I glared at him. "I didn't know this was going to be work."

"We don't have to paddle the entire way," he said, "just until we get past the houses."

"Can I take my mask off?" I said.

Hank chuckled. "The mask is for when we get to the marina, not now."

I perched at the port bow, and he paddled from the starboard stern. Once we passed the neighborhood, he yanked the starter rope several times. The engine answered with convulsive sputters, coughed billows of smoke, then finally caught with a roar, revving, then settling into an uneven thrum.

Looking embarrassed, Hank said, "She's a classic."

While he motored us northward, I spotted a red cooler tucked under the center bench of *Crime Cat*. Glad to see he'd brought refreshments, I opened it for a drink.

"Bruh!" It was filled with tools.

After a few minutes we were in sight of the marina and boatyard. Hank cut the engine off and we glided toward the boat ramp.

"See," I said. "This was so much faster than riding our bikes."

"Shh! Put your mask on."

Hank pointed at the boat ramp where someone was tying a small jon boat behind a larger pontoon boat secured to the finger pier that ran the length of the boat ramp.

"Quick, paddle over there!"

We made it to the shore, jumped out, and Hank pulled his boat up the embankment with his anchor rope.

I crouched down behind some brambles, but Hank climbed back aboard the boat with fluid precision and took something from his "toolbox."

He scampered beside me and raised a pair of binoculars to his eyes.

I watched the person—a man—board the larger boat and start the engines. They roared to life and he immediately shut them off, clearly stunned by the noise. The boat had a flat hull that rested on two large silver tubes that floated on the water.

"That's Emmitt," Hank whispered.

"Let me see."

He handed me the binoculars. The pontoon boat was stocked with red gas cans.

"What's he doing here after midnight on a pontoon boat with two 300-horsepower Kamaha engines?" Hank said.

"Isn't that what our boat had?"

"Yes—and it was overkill for a family pleasure boat. It's unusual—and I mean *extremely weird*—to see a pontoon boat with that much horsepower. Pontoon boats are designed for putzing around a lake or the ICW. It's the kind of boat you get if you have grandkids."

Emmitt untied the boat, pushed off from the pier, hopped aboard and began paddling like we had. The pontoon boat with the jon boat tied behind it took a lot more effort for him to get moving.

"Let's follow him," Hank said.

"No way," I said. "We're here for proof that one of the Fripps —and I think Emmitt is high on the list—worked with the thieves."

"Then let's be fast," Hank said. "If Emmitt continues to paddle, we might be able to catch up to him."

"And what are we going to do if we catch up to him?" I asked. "Conduct an interview? Ask if we can tag along?"

"We'll see where he's going." Hank put his mask on. "You remember where the security cameras are?"

"One at each end of the dock. Both aimed at the wet slips."

"Stick to the west edge of the dock to stay out of the camera field."

"How do I know which one is the west edge?" I asked.

He stopped what he was doing and gawked at me.

"What?" I asked.

"We live on the east coast of the United States. Do you know which way it is to the Atlantic Ocean?"

"It's that way." I pointed.

He raised his eyebrows. "Therefore, you can conclude…?"

I thought about it for a second, then realized how dumb I was. I aimed my thumbs over my shoulders and said, "West is that way."

Hank patted me on the head. "Good girl!"

We inched along the concrete retaining wall that ran the length of the marina's main dock, then up the gangway that sloped upward to the gate.

"We're going to have to climb it," Hank whispered, pointing to the chain link gate that separated the marina from the boatyard.

"I figured as much," I said, taking a pair of gloves out of the pocket of my hoodie.

"WhoDunnitHannah came prepared!" Hank said. "I'm going to forgive your geography brain fart."

"Thank you!" I said as I scaled the fence. The positive outcome from all that bike riding was visible in my leg strength.

Hank followed.

On the other side of the fence, a concrete walkway was bordered on the right by the marina store and on the left by more fence, about twenty feet long, that ended against the eastern wall of the dry stacks. Across the gravel lot was the gate that led to the boat graveyard.

"It looks like they still haven't installed the cameras on the dry stacks," Hank said, pointing upward. "That's good for us."

The forklift was parked in the corner of the gravel parking lot near the store. We climbed in the cab.

Papers were scattered on the dashboard along with someone's half-eaten lunch. "This thing is a pigsty," I said, pushing aside some burger wrappers. Under them was a clipboard with a list of owner names, boat brand names, descriptions, and slip numbers.

"Take a picture of that," Hank said.

I aimed my phone at the list and clicked.

Fanning through the pages, a smaller piece of note paper floated to the floor of the forklift.

I picked it up and shoved it in my pocket.

Hank grabbed a handkerchief that was sitting on the dashboard and stuffed it in his backpack. "This might have Emmitt's DNA on it. He seems to be the primary forklift operator."

"Stop right there and put your hands in the air!"

Hank and I turned slowly to see Old Mann Fripp standing next to the forklift with a long gun aimed at us.

"Um... uh..."

"Get off my forklift!" he shouted.

Hank climbed down first and then me.

"Take those masks off!"

We did as we were told.

Old Man Fripp gasped. "You two! You're the kids that got Chester Buckley fired!"

"That seems to be the mainstream interpretation," I said, "but actually his behavior got him fired, not ours."

"If you'd left well enough alone, we'd have more cops in the department and I probably wouldn't have got robbed!"

"I'm sorry, sir, but I don't think that's true," Hank said. "This appears to be the fourth in a rash of marina and boatyard robberies that began in July in Hilton Head."

We heard a siren in the distance.

"You called the cops?" I asked.

"Of course. I can't afford another break-in. I'm bleeding customers and money right now. People are pulling out of their slip rental contracts because they don't think my property is safe. I've been sleeping here at night since the robbery. That loud engine of yours woke me up!"

It wasn't our engine.

"We're really sorry, " Hank said, "but can you please call the cops back and tell them it was a false alarm?"

"Doesn't look like a false alarm to me!"

The siren grew louder.

"Mr. Fripp, my family's boat was stolen from here and I just wanted to see if we," I motioned to Hank, "can figure out who did it."

"If the cops can't figure it out, what makes you think you can?" he asked, lowering his gun slightly.

"Sir, we solved the Stacy McFarland disappearance thirty-five years after it happened," Hank said. "Officer Corker asked for our help."

"You expect me to believe he asked two kids to help him investigate a robbery? Did he tell you to trespass, too?" Mr. Fripp asked.

"No, we... sort of did that on our own," I mumbled.

The siren wailed.

"And that wasn't our boat engine that—"

Hank squeezed my elbow.

"Please, Mr. Fripp!" Hank pleaded. "I swear, we aren't here to do anything bad. We're just trying to put together a lot of odd pieces in this puzzle."

"Puzzle?" Fripp said. "This isn't a puzzle! This is my life! People broke into my business and stole a million dollar's-worth of stuff. Most of what they stole wasn't even mine. What was mine was insured, but I don't have insurance that will make the people of Vista Point trust me again. They're angry!" His voice cracked.

The blue lights turned the corner from Fripp Road onto Marina Lane.

"Please sir, don't turn us into the cops. We're getting really close to figuring out who robbed you!"

"Corker and Cantrell told me they don't have any leads."

"That's *them*," Hank said. "We've got several leads we still need to investigate."

Mr. Fripp's expression softened, and I think he honestly considered letting us go for a second or two. By then, the patrol car skidded up to the chain link fence. The cop got out and yelled, "Police! Put your hands in the air!"

30

HANK

In the state of North Carolina, first-degree trespassing occurs when a person enters an enclosed property without the owner's consent. Second-degree trespassing is when a person is caught entering someone's property that has a "no trespassing" or "private property" sign but is not enclosed. Some states, like Florida, allow a property owner to use or threaten to use force, but not deadly force, against another person to prevent them from trespassing. See Forensics 411 episode 12, "Crossing the Line."

"THIS IS CORKER. I need back up. I've got an armed assailant at Fripp's boatyard."

We put our arms down.

"Keep your hands up!" He yelled from the other side of the fence.

Mr. Fripp turned around. "It's me, Grady Fripp. I'm the one that called you!" He trudged toward the fence.

"Put the gun down!" Corker insisted, his voice quaking. "Stay where you are!"

Mr. Fripp set his gun on the ground in front of us and said, "Don't touch that!"

Hannah and I glanced sideways at each other.

"Should we run?" she whispered.

"Never a good idea to run from the cops."

Old Man Fripp opened the gate for Corker, who still had his gun drawn.

"Are those the burglars?"

"Yep."

Corker came closer, and the expression on his face changed.

"You two!" he said. "What the hell are you doing here?"

"They said they came here to investigate," Fripp said. "They say they have leads you don't have."

Oh, jeez, you didn't have to tell him that!

"Really!" Corker said. "Let's see what your parents have to say about you being out here in the middle of the night, trespassing on private property!"

"You said we could help with the investigation!" I interjected.

"Well... I... I didn't mean to trespass on private property. I just meant to look at the photos and see if you noticed anything—"

"And to interview the neighbors..." Hannah added.

Without even communicating with each other, we'd developed a strategy for how to handle the situation: make Corker look as guilty as we were.

"I never said to trespass!" Corker argued. "Oh, just you two wait 'til I take you home!"

He stopped talking and addressed Mr. Fripp. "Do you want to press charges?"

Fripp gave us a long stare. "I think it was just a misunderstanding," he said.

"Thank you," Hannah and I mumbled.

Corker inserted himself between Hannah and me and took each of us by the elbow. "Let's go!"

When we got to his patrol car, he put handcuffs on Hannah.

"Handcuffs?" I said. "Seriously? You know us. We weren't doing anything—"

"Except for criminal trespassing," Corker said as he cuffed me.

"It's only a misdemeanor," I said.

"Tell your mom that. I'm sure she'll be thrilled!" Corker griped.

THE RIDE to Hannah's house in the back of a patrol car reminded me of the last time we'd been in that situation. Over the summer, Agent Watts, Corker's SBI buddy, had driven us back to Hannah's house after we'd battled with Rodney Buckley.

"Seems like we've been in this position before," Hannah said.

"No handcuffs last time," I mumbled.

We rode in silence, and I wondered if she was thinking about what happened when Agent Watts dropped us at her house.

The kiss.

It wasn't a movie kiss, or even a TV kiss.

But it was a kiss just the same.

Neither of us had spoken of it since. (Not that we spoke of it *then*.) It was just something that happened. I knew we were going to be in a ton of trouble with our parents, and I silently wished that the reality of that would make her want to kiss me again—as if my lips gave her some sort of inner strength.

As we pulled in her driveway, she tapped my shoulder with her head.

"Good luck," I whispered.

"Oh, no!" Corker said. "You're not getting off that easy. I called your mom and she's on her way!"

"Here?" I groaned.

"Both of you—in the house!"

We didn't move.

"Let's go! In the house!" He flailed his arms at us like we were cattle.

"Um… Corker," I said gently. "We're handcuffed. And there's no handle on the door. We're gonna need a little help…"

"Oh, right."

Hannah and I rolled our eyes while he opened the car door for us.

"Move it!" Corker grunted.

"Steve," I used the familiar *Steve* to remind him that we were buds. "I don't think this is a good idea."

As Corker rang the doorbell, my mom pulled in the driveway.

"This is going to get ugly," I whispered to Hannah as Mom slammed her car door and marched across the lawn.

It took several rings before Hannah's mom finally came to the door.

"Hannah?" Mrs. Simmons gawked at her, then Officer Corker, then me, and finally at my mom who'd come up behind us. "What's going on?"

"Mrs. Simmons, I'm Officer Steve Corker. May we come in?"

"Uh-huh," she said. "Let me go wake up my husband."

Once we were in the living room, Corker took the cuffs off, and Hannah and I plonked beside each other on her sectional couch. Mom glared at me like she'd never glared before.

Mr. Simmons materialized in Sponge Bob pajamas. "What's going on here?"

"Grady Fripp caught Hank and Hannah trespassing at his boatyard," Corker said.

"What?" her dad said. "Trespassing?"

"Dad," Hannah said. "It's not what you think. Hank and I are helping Corker with the marina robbery."

"I received a call that trespassers had been spotted at Fripp's Boatyard. Fripp was worried he was getting robbed again."

"How did you get in?" Mr. Simmons asked.

"Climbed the fence," I said.

"Whoa!" Mrs. Simmons put her hands up. "Let me get this straight. You two were out at one o'clock in the morning climbing the fence to get into the boatyard that's, what, three miles away? You snuck out of the house?"

"Not quite two miles actually," I said. "And that's by land."

Hannah shook her head as if I'd said something wrong.

"And you did, too?" She pointed at me with a hostile finger.

"Uh-huh," I mumbled.

"And the other night, Hannah was in his bedroom!" Mom said. "She'd come through his window!"

"What!" Mrs. Simmons jumped to a standing position. "Are you kidding me? So... what? You sneak out all the time?"

"Not *all* the time," I answered.

"I'm not talking to you!" Mrs. Simmons growled at me.

"Hey!" Mom stood up, too, and aimed her finger at Mrs. Simmons. "Don't yell at my kid! Your *daughter* is the one crawling through my son's bedroom window!"

Mr. Simmons stood. "Ladies, ladies, ladies. I think we're missing the point here." He turned to Corker. "Officer, why *on earth* did you ask two fourteen-year-olds to help in your investigation?"

"Yeah!" Mom and Mrs. Simmons said in unison and turned their pointing fingers on him.

Corker was a deer in headlights.

I stole a look at Hannah. This was an unexpected twist. I hadn't considered that they'd turn on Corker.

"Uh..." His mouth hung open.

"I told you this would happen!" Mom poked him in the chest. "But no! You wouldn't listen to me. You were willing to put his safety in jeopardy so you could score points with him!"

"No!" Corker said. "That wasn't it at all."

"Yes, it was!" Mom poked him again. "You said you wanted to throw him a bone so he would like you!"

"I didn't think he'd break the law," Corker grumbled.

"It wasn't enough that he almost got killed by Rodney Buckley?" Mom squawked. "Why can't you think like an adult?"

"What?" Hannah's parents said.

"When did *that* happen?" Mrs. Simmons turned to Hannah. "Were you with Hank when he almost got killed?"

Clearly, Hannah hadn't told her parents about Rodney's attempt to kidnap her over the summer.

Hannah's eyes pleaded with me to help.

"She was fine. I knocked Rodney out with my boomerang. She had Corker's gun if she needed it."

"A *gun?*" Fault lines formed in Mr. Simmons' normally calm veneer.

Hannah shot me a look. "Good job!"

I put my hands up. "Look, let's just calm down." I tried to reassure Mrs. Simmons. "No, we don't sneak out *all* the time."

Hannah looked at Mom.

"The only reason I climbed through his bedroom window that night was because Hank was upset. That happens *when you withhold the identity of his father from him for fourteen years!*"

All I could think was *Oh no she didn't!*

"Mind your own business!" Mom glared at Hannah.

"Hey! Don't you yell at my daughter!" Mrs. Simmons gave my mom a little shove.

"Maybe she learned it from her pushy mother!" Mom said, shoving her back.

Mr. Simmons grabbed his wife and Corker grabbed Mom, trying to pull the women apart as they worked to get in each other's face.

"I'm just going to let them work this out," I said loudly enough that later, if necessary, I could legitimately and indignantly use the phrase *I told you I was leaving.* But quiet enough that none of the garrulous adults abandoned their thunderous moral platitudes to tell me to stay where I was.

"You are going to be in so much trouble!" Hannah whispered back.

"I'm going back for my boat. While you still have your phone, contact `Hacktivist77` through my website and ask him if he can get security footage from Coastal Freight Logistics the day that Roy Buck Denley rented the flatbed trailer."

"Tonight?"

"Do you think you'll still have your phone tomorrow?"

"Good point."

"If he can get the video, have him email it to you. Tell him I'll pay him later."

"You think he'll go for that?"

"Use your charm," I said.

LATER, Hannah texted while I motored south in *Crime Cat*: Sent message to H77. Haven't heard back. Ur mom is still here. They quieted down. Don't think any punches thrown.

I texted back: If anything happens to me, have Mom use Kid Tracker app on her phone. I installed it a few days ago.

31

HANNAH

T*edious (adj.) long, slow, dull, monotonous*

AT 2:50 THAT morning `Hacktivist77` messaged me back through the *Forensics 411* website.

`Link disappears in 3 min. after opened. Download. $100 when you solve the case. That's a bargain.`

The link said only `CFL83121.`

I downloaded it first, then emailed it to myself and Hank. It was highly unlikely that I'd have a phone for much longer, but I could always argue that I needed my laptop or tablet for school.

The link contained video of the lobby of Coastal Freight Logistics from August thirty-first. The camera was positioned behind the clerk who I assume handled the truck rentals. After I watched the video a few minutes, I concluded that I definitely did not want to be a clerk at Coastal Freight Logistics. Though there was no audio, I got the impression that most of their customers were angry at either the clerk or at life in general.

`Hacktivist77` had sent me twenty-four hours of video, which successfully put me to sleep fifteen minutes in.

32

HANK

R ecidivism is the tendency of convicted criminals to reoffend. Very few criminals commit only one crime. It is estimated that the most prolific burglars commit more than 232 burglaries per year. Police departments are finding that when they collect and analyze DNA from a burglary, they often get evidence that solves other cases as well. For more information on gathering evidence from a crime scene, see Forensics 411 episode 9, "Things Aren't Always What They Seem."

ONCE I RAN BACK to the marina for my boat, I motored home and slid in the house as quietly as possible. I grabbed a gallon of milk from the refrigerator, emptied it into the sink, and filled it with cold water. After dumping everything out of the main part of my backpack except for my army knife and latex gloves, I shoved in a box of crackers, a can of bug spray, a small plastic bowl, and my portable phone charger. Mom insisted I always have a charged phone.

In my bedroom, I woke Chaucer and put the leash on him.

"You have to be quiet," I told him. "We're going to be in a lot of trouble when Mom comes home, so we need to get as far away as possible. Stalk."

That was the command I gave Chaucer when I wanted him to be extra quiet. It was part of the search and rescue training we'd been working on.

We jogged down to the dock and hopped in *Crime Cat*. I didn't start the motor until we were all the way past Hannah's dock. The light was still on in her living room, so I assumed Mom was still there.

It was a rare windless night. Chaucer and I could hear the owl that lived in the hammock of trees across the water from Hannah's house. A deer leapt through the saltmarsh and I grabbed hold of Chaucer's collar before he could act.

"Don't even think about it!" I said, wrapping my other hand around his snout.

Chaucer whimpered as three more deer followed their leader through the marsh reeds.

We puttered down the waterway for a few miles before the smell of a campfire floated our way. I crossed the ICW from the mainland side to the saltmarsh islands that lay between it and the ocean.

I cut the engine and let *Crime Cat* drift. Unable to see through the dark shallow water and moonless night, I repeatedly scraped across oyster beds until I finally ran aground on a grassy flat.

"Stay," I told Chaucer.

I climbed out to push *Crime Cat* back into the water. As soon as my sneakers hit the grass, I sank shin-deep into the black marsh mud.

My attempt to lift one foot from the mud created a powerful suction that ripped my shoe off. I tried to snag it before it disappeared into the black abyss, and cut my arm all the way up to my elbow on oyster shells hiding in the mud.

"Chaucer, can you help me?"

He looked confused.

"Please?" I lifted my hand as if I were going to pet him.

He lowered his head, and I grabbed his collar with my right hand.

"Now back up."

He didn't have far to go on my five-foot-wide boat.

The foot that was still submerged in the mud budged slightly, creating a sucking sound that I felt sure someone heard.

Chaucer tried his hardest to pull me out of the mud. The wrinkles on his forehead were pushed forward by my holding his collar so tight.

"I'm sorry, boy. I know I'm hurting your neck. Just keep pulling."

He backed from port to starboard, then turned his body so his tail was toward the bow, giving himself more room to back up.

"You are so smart!"

As a team, I pushed and he pulled, and we finally got me out of the mud. But no shoes.

"Great," I mumbled. "Nothing like being shoeless on an oyster bed."

Chaucer looked at me as if to say *try being shoeless all the time!*

To get us off the flats, I repeatedly pushed my oar against an oyster bed on the opposite side of the grass flat, slowly nudging us back into water.

I only knew we were going to hit an oyster bed *after* we hit it. As a result, we plodded along at glacial speed. I intermittently commanded Chaucer to "stalk" just as a reminder that we had to keep quiet.

To the southeast, I saw the flames of the fire I'd been looking for.

I whispered to Chaucer, "Hannah would say *the campfire for which I'd been looking.*"

He snorted as if he got my joke.

I surveyed the island. On the northeast side was the back of a pontoon boat looking suspiciously like the one we'd seen Emmitt in earlier.

I reached under the seat for my binoculars.

The jon boat that had been tied to the back of the pontoon was gone. However, with two 300-horsepower Kamaha engines, and a cluster of red gas cans, it had to be the same pontoon.

A man with his back to me rolled up a sleeping bag. He was a tall figure wearing a camouflage t-shirt and jeans. That was not the clothing Emmitt had been wearing earlier. And though this person had a hoodie covering his head, I could tell he wasn't blond. He had a slight limp that I'd never noticed on Emmitt.

I paddled *Crime Cat* away from the man.

At the southern tip of the island, I spotted a small cove surrounded by wax myrtle. I paddled backwards to give *Crime Cat* a bit of a running start into the cove. I wanted to run the boat up onto the shore. With no shoes, jumping into the water to push it wasn't an option.

"Stay," I whispered to Chaucer. I gave my oar a giant shove to propel the boat onto the bank, slid out and stowed it under some vegetation.

I reminded Chaucer to stalk while I grabbed my backpack and his leash.

"Keep your head down," I said, as I pushed through shrubs strangled with vines and briars.

When we cleared the shrubs, my arms were stinging. The briars had carved a bloody roadmap into them.

Chaucer seemed to have fared better since I'd gone first and cleared the vines for him. "Good boy," I said. "You kept your head down."

The engines of the pontoon roared to life.

I crouched in the vegetation with my binoculars. The mystery man, seeming to recognize he was making too much noise, cut off one engine and moved through the water.

While he motored south, Chaucer and I crept deeper onto the island, heading toward the campfire three hundred yards to the north.

"Stalk."

We hid behind the dense vegetation as the pontoon passed us. I studied the driver through the binoculars. With the hoodie pulled over his head, I could only see the profile of his nose. I noted that the pontoon didn't have the registration numbers on the bow that boats usually had.

After the boat passed us, Chaucer and I trudged to the campsite.

With no wind, the no-see-ums and mosquitoes were out for blood—literally.

"I came prepared this time," I said to Chaucer as I doused myself in bug spray.

In the distance, I heard the second engine of the pontoon boat fire up.

As we got closer to the campfire, which the pontoon driver had failed to put out, I reached in my bookbag and palmed my army knife as if I could defend myself if necessary.

"Take a big whiff," I said as I held the handkerchief from the forklift in front of Chaucer's obedient nose. My best guess was that the handkerchief belonged to Emmitt and that he had delivered the pontoon to the island, then left in the jon boat. "Stalk."

Chaucer turned three circles then pointed in the direction of where the pontoon boat had been beached. I kept hold of the leash as his nose hit the ground. His head moved side to side, allowing his ears to waft the scents to his nose more efficiently. I tried to drag him to the campfire, but he was sure the scent trail led to the water.

When we arrived at the shoreline of the island, he sniffed in several directions trying to pick the scent back up. Then he sat. The scent was gone.

We moved to the campfire where I poured him some water in a small plastic bowl. He drank while I carefully searched the campsite area for clues about the identity of the camper.

The person had obviously not been a Boy Scout who learned to leave a campsite cleaner than he'd found it. Empty cans were scattered in the sand. He'd eaten a lot of beans, both kidney and baked. He was a fan of bottled beer and salty snacks. I counted twelve cans of beans, forty-eight bottles of beer and three empty bags of potato chips and concluded that our camper had spent more than one night on this little island. I slipped on latex gloves and stuck two beer bottles and an empty can of beans in my backpack.

I reached in my pocket for my phone to take pictures, but it wasn't there. I checked in my backpack.

"Shoot."

It was at least three in the morning. Mom would be home and fuming. I would be dead—at least figuratively—in the morning.

I threw sand on the campfire to put it out.

"Come on boy. This was a waste of time. I just tripled my punishment and have nothing to show for it."

We followed our tracks back to the boat. Before we ducked into the thicket, I reminded Chaucer to keep his head low.

I fought my way back through the stabbing briars and vines, giving my cuts and scrapes some cuts and scrapes of their own.

At the end of the prickly tunnel, I fell to the ground.

My boat was gone.

33

HANNAH

*I**ncarceration** (n.) confinement in jail or prison*

I WOKE Sunday to the sound of pounding rain on our metal roof. At the window, I studied the gray sky. Intermittently, a flash of lightning lit up the sky followed by a clap of thunder or a low rumble.

"I sure hope you made it home," I said to Hank, knowing he couldn't hear me.

My reckoning came around ten that morning. By that point, Mom and Dad were calm. That meant they'd taken the time to think things through and consult with each other to come up with the biggest and worst possible punishment—something that would really make me regret what I'd done.

There'd be some grounding, for sure. The question was how long.

My phone was a thing of the past. That was every parent's go-to punishment.

Would they take my allowance? Cut off my cash flow?

I stayed in my room and let them come to me. I'd have the

home advantage when the knock came.

"Hannah, we need to talk to you," Dad said.

Uh-oh. If Dad was taking the lead on this, it was bad. Mom was the disciplinarian. Dad usually just stood there and nodded while Mom told him what Josey or I had done, and then he'd look me squarely in the eye and say, *Do as your mother says*.

He opened the door and came in with Mom behind him.

She shot to my bathroom and ripped back the shower curtain. Next, she scurried across my room and lifted the dust ruffle on my bed.

"Looking for something?" I asked.

"Just want to make sure Hank isn't in here."

"Why would he be here?" I asked.

"His mother called and said he wasn't there when she got home last night. She can't find him anywhere," Dad said with genuine concern.

Whereas Mom lashed out with, "Do you know you could end up pregnant? Is that what you want?"

"What?" I shook my head. "How do you get pregnant from investigating a robbery?"

"Shh, shh, shh," Dad said squeezing Mom's shoulder. "Remember? We agreed we weren't going to do that. Let's all have a seat and act like we have some sense."

I held out my phone. "Here."

Mom snatched it from my hands and stuffed it in the pocket of her bathrobe.

"How long am I grounded for?"

"Hannah," Dad said calmly, "we were happy when you and Hank became friends, but now we're concerned about the negative influence he seems to have on you."

"You never snuck out of the house before you met him," Mom said.

"That's 'cause I was *eleven* the last time I had any real friends!"

"Remember when you hurt your ankle over the summer

chasing after his dog?"

"It wasn't even a sprain," I said. "Were we supposed to just let Chaucer die of heatstroke?"

"Now, we find out that you pulled a gun on someone." She clucked her tongue at me.

"Rodney Buckley! Am I not allowed to defend myself or Hank? Who knows what he would've done!" I argued. "And I didn't actually fire the gun. Agent Watts was the one who shot him in the leg!"

"So, we're supposed to be comforted by that?" Mom said.

"It wasn't *my* gun; it was Corker's."

"That's it!" Dad said pacing my bedroom. "That Corker seems to be at the root of all this trouble! He should've known that a gun needs to be locked up!"

"I think it's Hank that's dragged Hannah into all these messes," Mom said, "and I forbid you to see him ever again!"

I jumped up.

"No! That's not fair! He's my best friend!"

Dad shook his head slightly and murmured, "Jen, that's not what we discussed."

Mom snapped. "Do you want to lose *another* child?"

Dad bit his lip. "Of course, I don't want that," he said. "Let's stick to the script."

Mom stood up.

"Fine! You're grounded for two months. No phone. No allowance. And since you'll need to come straight home after school—no driver's ed!"

"What?" I stood up. "No! Please! I have to take driver's ed! I already signed up. If I give up my spot, I probably won't be able to take the class until the spring."

"Then that should give you plenty of time to sit at home and think about what you've done!" Mom said. "You brought this on yourself."

They left my room, and I threw myself backward onto my bed, kicked my mattress, and yelled, "I hate you!"

34

HANK

The term postmortem *is Latin for "after death." A* postmortem *exam is often called an autopsy and involves photographing the body; weighing and measuring it; doing a thorough external exam; searching for trace evidence; documenting any contusions or injuries; taking x-rays; and finally, dissecting the victim. The business world adopted the term* postmortem *to describe the process used by project participants to discuss what went right and wrong in the project. See* Forensics 411 *episode 7, "The Secrets of the Body," for a detailed description of the autopsy procedure.*

WITH MY BOAT GONE, I immediately regretted putting out the campfire.

Chaucer and I lay down on the sand. I used my backpack as a pillow, and Chaucer used me.

I rubbed his ears while I tried to figure out what to do. Someone had taken my boat, and my phone with it. The Kid Tracker app on Mom's phone wouldn't do her or me any good, but it would lead her to whoever stole my boat. It might even help us figure out the connection between Emmitt and the guy on the island.

I whispered, "Hannah, please remember what I told you about the app on Mom's phone."

Chaucer lifted his head at the mention of Hannah's name.

"No, sorry; she's not here."

He whimpered and let his chin fall back on my leg.

"At least I was smart enough to bring food and water."

I leaned forward and rubbed Chaucer's head. "Let's get some sleep."

The first rumble of thunder came as I closed my eyes.

I grasped Chaucer's collar in one hand, my backpack with the other, and scurried under a cluster of holly and myrtle as the first drops of rain pounded the island.

35

HANNAH

D *eprivation (n.) the damaging lack of material benefits considered to be necessities in a society*

"MOM?" I said from across the kitchen in my most gentle manner. "I need to call Ms. Boyd to tell her how she can find Hank."

"You know where he is?"

"No, but I can tell her how to figure it out. Can I use my phone?"

"No, I locked it in the safe for the next two months. Here," she handed me her phone. "You can use mine. Just hit *recent*. She was the last person to call me." Mom pointed to the kitchen floor. "You can stand right there to call."

I dialed her. "Hi, Ms. Boyd. It's me, Hannah. Have you found Hank?"

"No." She sniffled.

"Hank went back to the marina to get his boat last night and might have gone looking for Emmitt Fripp." I explained how we'd seen him earlier that night. "He told me to tell you that if he didn't come back or went missing, that he put an app on your phone called Kid Tracker. It tracks his cell phone, so you should be able to find him with that."

"Hang on. Steve's here. I need to tell him this." In a muffled voice I heard her say, "It's Hannah. She says Hank is in his boat. You need to get people out looking on the water, not just in patrol cars."

"Can you also tell Corker he needs to have someone looking for Emmitt Fripp in a pontoon boat towing a jon boat behind it? Emmitt is up to something. If he finds Emmitt, he might find Hank."

"I will. Thanks, Hannah."

I hung up and gave the phone back to Mom.

"Since that's taken care of, you are going to help your father clean the garage today."

Negotiation was fruitless.

36

HANK

M ost people know that eating raw oysters can be dangerous. One species of bacteria found in oysters, Vibrio vulnificus, can cause life-threatening wound infections. People with Vibrio vulnificus infections require antibiotics and some may need intensive care or limb amputations. See Forensics 411 episode 23, "Killing You Softly," for more information about deadly hazards in everyday life.

CHAUCER and I didn't sleep much. We gave up trying about an hour after the sun came up. Huddled under the wax myrtle, I took out the crackers and fed some to Chaucer one by one while the torrential rain slowly eased.

"Sorry I didn't bring any dog food, but I'll share these," I said. "They probably taste better anyway."

After six crackers, I slid the box in my backpack.

He whined and gave me the sad eyes.

"We need to ration... just in case. By now, Mom will have called the police. Hopefully, someone is out looking for us."

It was the Sunday of Labor Day weekend. Normally, the waters would be packed with boats. But not in the storm. I hadn't seen or heard a single boat. "We must be off the beaten path."

Chaucer sighed in agreement.

After we circumnavigated the entire island, I knew we were at least a few miles south of Vista Point. With the binoculars, I could see buildings on the mainland, but I didn't recognize any of them.

We returned to our makeshift campsite under the shrubs and watched the drizzle.

"I sure hope they're out looking for us," I told Chaucer, "because without my shoes, I don't know how we'll get home. We could swim out and hope that someone sees us, but this island is surrounded by oyster beds. We can't get out to water that's deep enough to swim in without doing some damage."

37

HANNAH

N ostalgia (n.) a sentimental longing or affection for the past, typically for a period or place with happy personal associations

SINCE WE'D ONLY LIVED in our house for three months, the garage wasn't even that messy. Mom just wanted to punish me. Dad only needed me to help him hang some shelves for the boxes we hadn't bothered to open when we moved from Pittsburgh. Most of them were Ben's things.

Mom had decorated the bedroom in the lower-level in-law suite with Ben's Steelers bedspread and posters from our old house. She put his trophies on the shelf with all his favorite books. It was as if he were gone away to summer camp, not *gone,* gone.

Tears welled up in my eyes.

Dad saw it, took the box from me, and whispered, "I know."

He set the box on the ground. "Come over here and hold the brackets while I put the screws in."

We worked in silence for a few minutes.

"Dad, I'm really worried about Hank. I know you don't want to hear it, but we felt like we were getting close to an answer in the robbery case. We think maybe Emmitt Fripp, Mr. Fripp's son, was purposely moving the more valuable boats to the bottom row of the dry stacks so that someone could steal those particular engines and electronics."

"An inside job?"

"Yeah." I told him about the video doorbell, the red truck, and Coastal Freight Logistics. "I need to finish watching the security camera footage."

Dad stopped with the drill and stared at me in disbelief. "Hank has a hacker friend who stole a local business's security camera footage and sold it to you?"

"Well, when you put it that way…"

He aimed the drill at me. "Do you know that what you did is illegal?"

I shrugged my shoulders. "I mean, I guess so."

"Hannah, your actions have real consequences… bad consequences."

"At this point, there's no turning back," I said. "And we need to find Hank."

"Can't you just read a mystery rather than investigate one?" Dad said. "Corker should never have included you in his police work."

"Could you call Officer Corker and see if he's found Hank yet?"

"I don't want you involved. Period."

Dad and I finished hanging the shelves and piled the boxes onto them. One was labeled CLOTHES. I used a box cutter to open it. Inside, were Ben's *Star Wars* pajamas, a lot of clothes that Mom called *school clothes*, and a tiny number eighty-six Steelers jersey with WARD written across the shoulders. Hines Ward was my dad's favorite Steeler.

I held the football jersey to my nose, hoping to smell his typical nine-year-old-boy-right-after-playing-outside scent. I used to call it his *boy stink*.

I inhaled and was briefly transported back to a simpler time in my life where I didn't know that people like Helen Tate and Jackson-whatever-his-last-name-was existed. A time when my little brother was bugging the crap out of me and I would tell him to go away and leave me alone.

But now, that's what he'd done... gone away and left me alone.

I handed the Steeler's jersey to Dad and took the *Star Wars* pajama top for myself.

"I'll get some tape upstairs," Dad said.

He came back a minute later with the tape. "Where's this video surveillance you were telling me about?"

"It's in my email. I only watched fifteen minutes before I fell asleep."

"Well, I think we can both agree you had quite the day yesterday. Why don't we go to the library, and you can use the computers there?"

"Really?" I hugged him.

"I am in the same camp as your mother about not wanting you in danger, but I know you're worried about Hank. I'll help you this time, but Mom and I would really like you to find another hobby."

I ran upstairs, changed clothes, and tucked Ben's pajama top in the back of my sock drawer.

Dad told Mom he was taking me to the library to get a book for a school project. He promised to not let me out of his sight.

NOT ONLY DID Dad take me to the library, he sat at the computer next to me and helped me watch the Coastal Freight Logistics security feed. I started at the beginning and fast-forwarded in-between customers while Dad started at the end of the tape and rewound. Each time a customer's face could be seen, we took screen shots and sent them to my email.

When we were done, Dad's phone rang.

"Hello. Yes. This is John Simmons," he said. "Oh, hi, Officer Corker."

I stood up and put my ear next to Dad's phone to hear Corker say, "I got a call from a marina owner in Georgia who thinks he saw your boat. Someone was taking it out of the water and putting it on a trailer."

"Did he get a license plate?"

"No, but I've had Marcia contact the South Carolina, Georgia and Florida DOTs and highway patrols to be on the lookout for the boat being towed."

"Okay, good."

"Is Hannah with you?" Corker asked.

"I'm here."

"Hannah, someone found Hank's boat in the saltmarsh south of Wilmington. The engine was missing, and the inside was covered in marsh mud.

"Was Chaucer in the boat?"

"No."

"Good."

"Why is that good?" Corker asked.

"Hopefully, that means Hank and Chaucer are together. They won't let anything happen to each other. Does his mom know?"

"Not yet. Cantrell's getting the boat from the Coast Guard and is going to tow it up to her house with the department boat. I'm going to drive up there to tell her in person. Don't worry. We'll find him."

"Have you questioned Emmitt Fripp?"

"No. Apparently, he scheduled this as a vacation day a few weeks back, and nobody knows where he is."

"He scheduled it *weeks* ago?" I asked. That could mean his "disappearance" was premeditated.

"What about Brock?"

"I called him. He said Emmitt had a date last night and never came home."

"Did you ask Brock if he knew anything about the pontoon or jon boat?"

"Emmitt has a jon boat he usually keeps on a trailer at their house. He took it out yesterday evening to go fishing before his date. Brock doesn't know anything about a pontoon boat," Corker said. "Do you have reason to believe the pontoon boat is related to the robbery or Hank's disappearance?"

"Well... yeah... sort of. Hank went out on his boat to look for the pontoon that Emmitt was driving. So maybe if we find the pontoon, we'll find Hank." Wondering whether Hank would tell Corker or not, I added, "We think Emmitt might be involved in the robbery."

"What? Do you have evidence?"

"We have strong suspicions," I said, knowing suspicions weren't good enough. "Could you ask Marcia to see if she can find records on a person named Roy Buck Denley?"

"Roy Buck Denley? Who's that?"

"He's the person who rented the flatbed trailer with the red cargo container on it that showed up at the marina the night of the burglary. We told you about it," I said.

"Wait. I thought you didn't have a license plate?"

"We didn't... but now we do."

"How?" Corker asked.

"Well... there's a few things related to the case that you don't know about."

I could hear him take a deep breath.

"Tell me...."

"It's kind of more like *show me*," I said.

"Elaborate."

"Maybe my dad will let me come see you at Hank's house."

I questioned Dad with my eyes.

He ran his hand across his head. "This is going to get me in trouble with your mom, isn't it?"

"Not if we don't tell her."

"Fine," Dad said. "But check out a couple books so we can prove we were really here."

I dashed to the nearest shelf, picked up two books, checked them out, and met Dad in the car.

"Well?" Dad said with a mischievous smile, "What did you get to read?"

I read the titles for the first time.

"Ugh," I said. *"Clinical Care of the Diabetic Foot* and *The Salon Professional's Guide to Hands and Feet."*

Dad chuckled. "Toes!"

38

HANK

C hildren playing or experimenting with fire set more than 20,000 fires each year. Kids between five and ten years old are most likely to play with fire. Accidental fires started by children cause an average of 150 deaths and nearly 1,000 injuries per year. See Forensics 411 *episode 15, "Fired Up," to learn more about fires, both accidental and arson.*

BY AFTERNOON, the rain let up and I was able to gather wood for a fire.

I hadn't seen a boat all day.

I came back with some dryish twigs, pine needles and bark from a river birch. Under the vegetation, I dumped the contents of my backpack in the sand: two empty beer bottles, an empty can of beans, a box of crackers, a can of bug spray, my cell phone charger and the plastic water bowl. My army knife had a screwdriver, a tiny saw, miniature scissors, tweezers, pliers, and a knife. In the front zipper pocket of my backpack was a tube of lip balm, two pencils, a little packet of tissues, and a pack of gum with three sticks in it.

I chewed a stick of the gum and stared out at the island, really hating myself for putting out that campfire.

I glanced at Chaucer. "I blame Smokey Bear for my fire safety habits."

He lifted his head in agreement.

I replaced the contents of my backpack, gathered up all the beer bottles and bean cans the camper had left behind, and piled them under our shelter of shrubs.

I stripped the bark off the kindling using several different tools from my army knife. The wood underneath was relatively green which meant it wouldn't make much heat, but it would make smoke.

Rubbing Chaucer's ears, I said, "It's September in North Carolina. I don't think we're at risk of hypothermia. I opt for smoke."

Chaucer begged for dinner in the late afternoon, and I obliged with six crackers, feeding them to him one at a time.

While he ate, I thought about one of my favorite childhood books. The main character, Brian, was a twelve-year-old boy who survived a plane crash in the woods of Canada with nothing but a hatchet. After much consideration, I realized I had several advantages over Brian: I had forty-eight beer bottles and cans of beans. Though empty, they all had paper labels. Paper was flammable. Unlike Brian who had no idea where he was in Canada, I was in sight of civilization. Though I didn't have my cell phone, I did have my portable cell phone charger, my army knife and bug spray. Cell phones hadn't even been invented when Brian was marooned.

While I peeled the labels off the cans and bottles, I considered one of my eighth grade vocabulary words: *Conflagration*.

Somebody was out looking for me, and hopefully the smoke from any fire I could build would draw them in my direction like the pontoon man's fire had drawn me.

I cut the silver gum wrapper into strips with my mini scissors. Next came the battery from my portable cell phone charger.

Nearby, I had built a small teepee of kindling. Beside that were pine needles, bark, the tissues, my stick of lip balm and the two pencils. I also cut Emmitt Fripp's handkerchief into long strips and was prepared to burn my backpack if necessary.

I pressed the end of one strip of the foil against the terminals of the battery with the metal pliers from my army knife and waited for the gum wrapper to burst into flames...

Nothing happened.

39

HANNAH

Deductible *(n.) a North American term used to describe a specified amount of money that an insured person or business must pay before an insurance company will pay on an insurance claim*

DAD and I arrived at Hank's house the same time as Officer Corker.

He knocked on the door, and the three of us waited awkwardly while no one answered.

"Maybe she's in the shower. I'll give her a call," Corker said.

He left a message.

"Angie, it's Steve. I'm at your house. Give me a call as soon as you get this."

Minutes later, Officer Cantrell pulled up to the dock on the police department boat, with *Crime Cat* in tow.

We went down to meet him.

"Was Hank's cell phone on the boat?" I asked Officer Cantrell, then looked at Corker. "You told everyone about the Kid Tracker app, right?"

"Yes."

"No cell phone on the boat." Officer Cantrell peered uneasily at Corker. "Can I talk to you in private?"

"Sure."

They stepped away, and I climbed aboard the boat and opened the red cooler that Hank used as a toolbox.

"What are you looking for?" Dad asked.

"A clue," I said rummaging through the tools. "His binoculars aren't in here."

"Okay?" Dad said. "Is that important?"

"He was using them last night at the marina."

"Hannah?"

I turned to Officer Corker.

"The Coast Guard tracked Hank's cellphone to the bottom of the Cape Fear River, south of downtown Wilmington."

I rubbed my hand between my thumb and index finger. "Did they find his body?" I asked, sounding much more mature, clinical, and detached than I felt.

"No."

"Okay, then he's fine. He's alive... somewhere. He just got separated from his phone and his boat. He's with Chaucer."

Corker's phone rang.

"Hey, Angela," he said. "I'm at your house with Hannah and her dad. Where are you?"

He listened. "Oh? I didn't realize the Coast Guard called you." He shook his head. "No. It doesn't mean he's dead. It just means he got separated from his phone and his boat. He and Chaucer are probably together. Don't stay there and watch the divers. It'll only upset you more. Come home. Hannah has some things she wants to show me that might help us find him."

That wasn't exactly true. It was more like information that would help him figure out who robbed Fripp's boatyard. If we went on the assumption that Hank's disappearance was connected to the person on the pontoon boat, and the pontoon boat was connected to the robbery, and the hip bone was connected to the thigh bone, then *maybe* I had useful information. That was a lot of *ifs*. Hank would call it circumstantial evidence, but it was better than no evidence at all.

Corker got his laptop from his car, and we went in the house to wait for Hank's mom.

Inside, I called out to Hank's grandpa to let him know we were there.

"He's with Angela," Corker said. "You know, since he's been roaming."

In Hank's bedroom, I grabbed the case notebook from his dresser. Then we all sat at the kitchen table while I logged into my email from Corker's laptop.

"Eugene Lund, the man who lives at the corner of Marina Lane and Fripp Road has a video doorbell. We took screenshots of all the walkers, bikers and vehicles that activated the camera on Monday and Tuesday," I pointed to the screen. "Hank has a friend who's good with photos and technology. He was able to clear up the pictures. The cab of the red truck didn't have any writing or DOT numbers on it. But he got the license plate." I read the plate number from our notes.

"The flatbed trailer is part of a rental fleet that's registered to a company in Indiana, but it made its way to Wilmington. The flatbed trailer and a cargo shipping container were rented from Coastal Freight Logistics on Monday by someone named Roy Buck Denley. That's why I wanted Marcia to check on him."

"Marcia checked," Corker said. "There's no record of a Roy Buck Denley anywhere. She checked all fifty Departments of Motor Vehicles and the FBI's database. So, either Roy Buck Denley doesn't have a driver's license, has no criminal record, or he's from a foreign country."

"Wouldn't he have to present a driver's license to rent a fleet truck?" my dad asked.

"Good point." Corker nodded as if impressed by my dad's suggestion.

"So probably Roy Buck Denley is an alias," Dad said, "and he used a fake license."

I gave Dad my own approving nod. He was getting the hang of this investigation stuff.

"Hank and I think that maybe the Fripps purposely moved the boats with more valuable engines and equipment down to the bottom row of the dry stacks. Just a sec and I'll show you why."

I darted to Hank's closet to get the chart we'd made. In the shoe box, I spotted the cigarette butts and grabbed those too. Underneath the zipper bag lay pieces of his rubber foam ball... his comfort object. I picked up a small chunk, gave it a squeeze, then put it back. "Don't worry. We're going to find you. I promise."

"Here." I handed him the chart. "We had four different sets of pictures of the dry stacks." I explained the origins of each set of photos. "We made this chart documenting which boats were in the fifteen slips on the bottom row in each of the four sets of pictures."

Corker studied our work.

"As you can see, Emmitt and Brock have been moving boats around a lot. The only thing we could figure about the method to their movements was that they put boats with high horsepower Kamaha engines on the bottom row, even ones with only one Kamaha engine. They also put boats with valuable electronics on the bottom row." I explained how I'd seen Emmitt and Brock move the bright green boat on Monday.

"That boat belongs to Lacy and Dan Garfield," Corker said. "She told me her boat is usually stored in D-12 and she had no idea why it was on the bottom row the night of the robbery. They had a ten-thousand-dollar sound system in that boat."

"Did you notice that the thieves didn't take the 250-horse-power Johnston engine on it? That goes along with what Hank said about the professional thieves only wanting high-horse-power Kamaha engines."

"So wait," Corker said. "You think Grady was working with the thieves?"

"We're not sure. He seems genuinely upset about how he's lost the trust of his customers because of the robbery. He had to have foreseen that happening if he decided to steal from them."

"Maybe he did it for the insurance money?" Corker said.

"Hank thought about that, but Mr. Fripp didn't have anything to gain from an insurance scam. The only things insured on his policy that got stolen were the electronics from the shop. Mr. Calhoun had purchased those with company money."

"But that was close to a hundred grand in equipment."

"He'd have to pay his deductible on the stolen items he owned," Dad said. "So, he'd be out that money even if he stole all the other items himself," Dad said. "And then he'd still have to replace the equipment taken from the shop. If it was an insurance scam, it wasn't a good one."

I didn't know what a deductible was, but I trusted Dad when it came to his knowledge of insurance.

"Well, whatever cash he lost to the deductible could've been worth it for him. Close to a million dollar's-worth of stuff was stolen," Officer Corker said. "And Fripp wouldn't be paying to replace all his customers' engines and electronics. That would be their responsibility. So once Grady Fripp sold all the stolen equipment, he'd still come out good."

Hank's mom and grandpa came in.

She ran to us with her arms open. I thought she was going to hug Corker, but instead she wrapped her arms around my shoulders.

It surprised me, considering how mad she'd been at me the night before.

"Oh, Hannah! Thank you for coming!"

"What about the screen shots we took of the truck rental place?" Dad asked.

"Oh, ya," I said, gently pulling away from Hank's mom. I found the file with the screen shots from the Coastal Freight Logistics security video and turned it back for Corker to see.

Mr. Boyd went to the refrigerator and came back with a block of cheese, a plate, and a knife. He sliced a few pieces of cheese.

He studied me and said, "Did you know Hannah is an anagram?"

"Actually, it's a palindrome," I said. "An anagram is when letters are rearranged to make a new word—"

"Like Adam and Amad," Mr. Boyd said.

"Yes," I said. "A palindrome is when a word is spelled the same forward or backwards, like *mom, pop,* or *dad.*"

"Dad," Ms. Boyd pleaded, "why don't you go eat somewhere else so we can work here at the table."

"Fine!" Hank's grandpa stormed off to the den.

"Sorry about that," Ms. Boyd said. She turned to Officer Cantrell. "He has dementia."

Officer Corker studied the screenshots from the security video. "Tell me again how you got these photos?" Corker asked.

"A friend of Hank's," I said.

"Should I know more than that?" he asked.

"Nope."

Corker shook his head in disgust. "Any evidence you acquire illegally is inadmissible in court."

I held my own and calmly said, "Without us there wouldn't *be* any evidence."

I surveyed the adults in the room waiting for one of them to "put me in my place," but no one said a thing.

Corker went back to the ill-gotten security footage.

"Well, well, well. Look what the cat dragged in! There's Rodney Buckley at Coastal Freight!"

I gasped. "Rodney Buckley was there?"

"Yep," Corker said. He showed me a photo that I hadn't seen. Rodney must have been in the part of the security video Dad watched.

I considered that for a moment, then jumped up and ran to Hank's desk for some paper and a pencil.

Back at the table, I wrote the name Roy Buck Denley on a

piece of paper and studied the letters. One by one, I crossed them out. "It's an anagram!" I said. "Roy Buck Denley is Rodney Buckley! We need to find out if he rented the flatbed trailer that was used to haul everything away from the burglary at Fripp's!"

"Hang on, there," Corker said. "We still don't know that the truck had anything do with the burglary, and we don't know what Rodney Buckley was doing at this rental place." Corker shrugged. "He might've just been looking for a new vehicle to live in since he burned his school bus."

I scoffed. "Yeah, because we know what an up-standing citizen Rodney Buckley is!"

I waved my hands around trying to waft some sense in Corker's direction. "Isn't it obvious? Rodney *must* be part of the boatyard burglary. It's too much of coincidence for him to show up at the same business that rented the flatbed truck that was seen at the boatyard the night of the robbery. He might've figured out that we were on to him and went after Hank."

"But you *weren't* on to him until just now," Dad said.

I sank into the chair. Dad was right.

"I'll call Coastal Freight," Cantrell said, "and find out what Roy Buck Denley rented and get a copy of the license he used to rent the truck." He headed to the back door but then stopped and turned around. "You know, Rodney, Emmitt, Brock and I all graduated from high school together," Officer Cantrell said. "Back then, Rodney and Emmitt were pretty tight."

I glared at Corker. "Another coincidence?"

40

HANK

Many scholars believe that early humans were able to control fire dating back as far as 1.7 to 2 million years ago. Being able to start and control fire allowed for cultural advances because fire created warmth, lighting, protection from predators, and allowed for cooking and more advanced hunting tools. See **Forensics 411** episode 15, "Fired Up," for more details.

I STARED at the phone charger battery, foil, and my pliers.

"Come on!" I growled at the gum wrapper. "You're supposed to catch fire! Didn't you pay attention is seventh grade science?"

I exchanged that strip of foil for one of the others, wiped off the battery terminal and pliers with my t-shirt and tried again. This time wishing with all my heart that I had an amateur arsonist in me.

The energy stored in the battery should've—

Burst into flame!

"Yes!"

I leaned over and lit a beer bottle label on fire, followed by a can label. I placed them under the teepee of kindling and added pine needles, one at a time so I didn't create an air draft that would extinguish my tiny flame. As that caught, I added the bark from the river birch tree, then more pine needles.

"I did it, Chaucer! I made fire!"

He celebrated my achievement with a jubilant howl.

One by one, I added twigs, then the kindling I had stripped of its bark. After about twenty minutes, when it was solidly burning, I added an actual log.

It was dinner time, and we had fire!

41

HANNAH

I **nquisition** *(n.) a period of prolonged and intensive questioning or investigation*

I HELD the plastic bag of cigarette butts up for Corker to see.

"We still have these from the boatyard. Are you sure you don't want to test them for DNA?"

Before Corker could balk at the idea of spending department money to actually solve a case, Hank's mom said, "I'll pay for it myself!"

Ms. Boyd snatched the bag of cigarette butts out of my hand and handed them to Corker. "Do it. Please. For me."

Officer Cantrell came back in. "Just talked to the owner of Coastal Freight Logistics. Roy Buck Denley used a CDL driver's license from Idaho to rent a flatbed trailer and cargo container on Monday afternoon. He hooked them up to what the Coastal Freight clerk called an 'old school cab.' The owner texted me a picture of the license, and it's definitely Rodney Buckley's face."

"I'll put out an APB," Corker said.

"What about Emmitt?" I said.

"Let's go to the marina and see if we can talk to a Fripp... any Fripp."

Dad and I followed Corker to the boatyard in our own car. While Dad drove, I reached in the pocket of my shorts—the same pair I'd worn the night before. For the first time, I studied the note paper that had fallen from Emmitt's clipboard in the forklift. It appeared to be three columns of boat slip numbers.

THE DOOR WAS open to Mr. Fripp's office, but Corker knocked anyway.

Old Man Fripp glanced up from his computer screen. "You got good news?"

"We need to talk to Emmitt," Corker said.

"He's off today. He's lucky it's raining because that boy knows better than to take off on a holiday weekend. What's goin' on?"

"Grady, Rodney Buckley rented a flatbed trailer and shipping container down in Wilmington on Monday."

"Am I supposed to care what that little turd's up to?" Fripp asked.

"Your neighbor, Eugene Lund, has a video doorbell," I said, "and he caught that same red eighteen-wheeler driving toward the marina on Monday evening about eight-thirty, and leaving at two-twenty early Tuesday."

"Was anyone still here at eight-thirty Monday night?" Corker asked.

"No. I left earlier than usual because it was mine and Darlene's anniversary. We went out to dinner down in Wilmington. Emmitt and Brock locked up. We close at seven or dusk, whichever comes first."

"Who has keys to the locks at the boatyard?" Corker asked.

"Me, Emmitt, Brock, and Darlene."

"May we see your security footage from last night—at about midnight?" Corker asked.

"Last night?" Mr. Fripp pointed to me. "That's when those kids were snoopin' around."

"Yes," Corker said. "I'd like to see the footage of the camera aimed at the boat ramp."

Mr. Fripp spun the desktop computer around, then typed something on his keyboard.

"Hmm," Mr. Fripp said. "Only the farthest camera at the gate into the boatyard seems to be working. That's weird. It would've been charged this week. Darlene has a schedule for the boys to follow."

According to the time stamp on the video, at 12:38, a person wearing a dark hoodie and brown pants pulled up to the fuel dock in a jon boat filled with gas cans. He climbed out of the boat and, one by one, filled each can, then carried it out of the field of the camera.

I heard Mr. Fripp grunt.

"Do you recognize that person?" Corker asked.

"It's hard to see. He's got a hood over his head, and the picture is grainy." Mr. Fripp said.

"Do you lock your gas pumps?" Corker asked.

"Of course, I lock my pumps."

"Who has keys to the fuel pumps?"

"Me, Emmitt, Brock, and my wife—same people who have keys to the gates and the store. This is a family operation. We only leave the pumps unlocked when one of us is tending the fuel dock. Otherwise, we'd have people comin' up here stealing gas and diesel all the time."

"Did you see this person in the jon boat unlock the pumps?" Corker asked.

"I don't know. Let me watch again." Mr. Fripp turned the computer back around, typed on the keyboard and re-watched the security footage. His shoulders slumped. "Looks like he unlocked the pump."

"And if that's Emmitt, he would've known to disable the security camera closest to the fuel dock and boat ramp," I said.

"Emmitt? What makes you think that's Emmitt?"

"You just said there are only four of you with keys to the pumps, and that's clearly not you or your wife in the video," Corker said. "It's one of your sons."

"Maybe someone took the keys from Emmitt or Brock," Mr. Fripp said.

We continued to watch the person fill up gas cans from the jon boat and carry them out of the field of the camera.

"Mr. Fripp, Hank and I got to the boat ramp around one o'clock. At that point, there was a pontoon boat with two 300-horsepower Kamaha engines loaded with red gas cans." I pointed to his computer screen. "That jon boat was tied to the back of it. When you caught us last night, you said that our boat engine woke you, but it wasn't us. It was the pontoon's engines."

I tried to not sound accusatory. "Hank and I *saw* Emmitt ride off in the pontoon boat, towing the jon boat behind it. He wasn't wearing that hoodie when we saw him, and it was definitely him. He started the engines, realized how loud they were, and cut them off. He used oars to push off from the dock and paddle south. Later that night, after you called the cops on us, Hank came back here to get his boat, and he was going to see if he could catch up to Emmitt on the pontoon boat."

"Currently, Hank is missing," Corker said.

"You're telling me that, in the middle of the night, my son stole gas from me, loaded it onto a pontoon boat, and left?" Mr. Fripp said. "The boy followed him, and now the boy's missing?" He shook his head. "Emmitt's sneaky enough to take gas without paying me for it, but he's no kidnapper."

"Can we talk to Brock?" Corker said.

"He's outside," Mr. Fripp pointed.

∼

BROCK WAS SITTING in the forklift with the engine off.

"Come on down here, Brock," Mr. Fripp said. "We need to ask you some questions."

Brock stepped down from the forklift, looking confused.

"What was Emmitt up to after work yesterday?" Mr. Fripp asked.

"He said he had a date with that girl he's been seeing. We went home and he took a shower. Ate dinner. He took his boat out to fish for a little bit until he was supposed to meet that girl when she got off work at ten. He never came home, and I ain't seen him since."

"What's this girl's name?" Corker asked.

"He won't tell me. She seems mighty possessive 'cause she made him get a separate cell phone just for her to call him on."

"Really?" Corker said. "That seems odd."

Brock nodded. "I thought so, too. I think maybe she's married and running around on her husband."

"What do you know about this?" I handed Brock the note paper with the list of slip numbers that I'd found on the forklift clipboard the previous night.

"That's the list we worked from on Monday. Pop gave it to Emmitt."

Mr. Fripp snatched the list from Brock's hands.

"I didn't give him this. I've never even seen it before!" Mr. Fripp said. "What'd he tell you it was for?"

"He said you told him to move some boats around 'cause you were reassigning slips," Brock said. "We moved them all on Monday. These ones in the left column were the boats on the bottom row that we moved to a higher slip. And the ones in the middle column were the ones we moved into the bottom slips that we emptied out. Then the ones in the right column were the ones that were already on the bottom row and we kept 'em there." He looked at his father. "Emmitt said you wanted it done before we went home for the day. 'Course, then on Tuesday,

Emmitt said you changed your mind and wanted us to move them back."

Mr. Fripp scoffed.

"Speaking of Monday evening, Emmitt's truck wouldn't start, right?" Officer Corker asked.

"Uh-huh."

"You two usually ride to work together, right?" I asked.

"Yep. But we'd taken separate cars that day 'cause he was supposed to meet up with that girl after work." Brock shrugged. "When his truck wouldn't start, we just took mine home. "

"Did he see his girlfriend after work?" Officer Corker said.

"No. I mean, he couldn't 'cause he had to leave his truck at work," Brock said.

"Did you drive him into work on Tuesday morning?"

"Yep. When we got here, his truck was over at the boat ramp. I guess the thieves got it started."

"That was my boat on the trailer that was stolen," my dad said.

"She sure was a beauty," Brock said. "I feel awful for all the folks who had stuff stolen."

"Did Emmitt bring his jon boat back to the house last night before his date?" Corker asked.

"No. Like I said, he ain't been back to the house since he left to go fishing. That was about eight-thirty last night."

"Do you know the phone number of the phone he uses to call his girlfriend?" Officer Corker asked.

Brock shook his head. "Nah."

"What about Rodney Buckley?" Corker asked. "Have you or Emmitt seen or heard from him lately?"

"He's been coming around a bit lately. Last time he was over at the house was last Sunday."

"What did he want?" Corker asked.

"I don't know. He only talks to certain people, and I ain't one of them. He's always been more Emmitt's friend than mine.

They went outside for a while, had a couple beers, then Rodney left."

"Have you seen a pontoon boat around? One with two 300s on it?" Mr. Fripp asked.

"A pontoon with two 300s?" Brock laughed. "Shoot! Why would anyone put that much power on a pontoon boat?"

"Have you seen one?" Mr. Fripp asked, impatiently.

"No."

"Brock, did Emmitt ever have trouble with his truck starting before Monday?" I asked.

"Nope. For as much as he paid for that truck, he ought not to have any trouble out of it."

"Does Emmitt usually lock his truck when it's here during the day?" I asked.

"Yeah."

"Did he have his keys with him when you drove him home on Monday?"

Brock stared out at the water for a second, seeming to think about it.

"Now that you mention it, no. When we pulled in the driveway, I went in the backyard to feed Scooby Joe—that's our dog. Emmitt said he forgot his keys at work 'cause he was so mad about the truck not starting."

"Did he find his keys on Tuesday when you went into work?" I asked.

"He thought he'd left them in the office, but when we got in on Tuesday, it turns out he left them in his truck."

I flashed a look at Officer Corker. "Interesting."

Mr. Fripp studied the ground.

"Can you think of anything unusual about Emmitt's behavior right before or after the robbery?" Corker asked.

Brock shook his head. "Is Emmitt in some kind of trouble?"

"We don't know at this point, but we really need to find him," Corker said, handing him a business card. "If you hear from him, let me know."

42

HANK

A rson is the willful or malicious burning of property, especially *with criminal or fraudulent intent. Studies show that approximately twenty percent of wildfires are caused by arson. Only four percent of structure fires are started by arsonists. For more information on arson, see* Forensics 411 *episode 43, "Burning for You."*

As THE DAY WENT ON, I decided to end my previously cordial relationship with Smokey the Bear. It was my best hope for getting rescued.

I rubbed lip balm on the paper-like river birch bark and added a piece to the fire. Since lip balm was petroleum-based, it caught fire quickly. I slathered more pieces of the bark and tossed them in as well.

Next, I took one of the logs that I had peeled the bark off.

Chaucer tilted his head from left to right, trying to understand what I was doing.

"Just watch," I said, letting go of his leash. "And back up."

I coated the log in bug spray and threw it into the campfire.

Whoosh! The flames came alive.

Piece by piece, I covered more logs with the very flammable bug spray and added them to the fire.

The smoke I'd wanted was forming. Someone would see it or smell it soon.

I was concentrating on the flames when Chaucer let out a series of urgent barks. My dog howled, yelped, and whined, but he seldom expressed himself in barks.

"What's wrong?" I glanced down beside me where he had just been, but Chaucer was gone.

I dropped the bug spray and followed his frantic barks.

"Chaucer! Come!" I shouted, walking more briskly.

Between his barks, I heard screams, growls, and hisses.

The smoke from the campfire grew and followed me.

Chaucer's barks had turned to cries when I found him.

He stood frozen but made sounds like a wild coyote. Six feet in front of him was a raccoon, hissing, snarling, and aggressively biting at the air.

I grabbed the largest limb I could find.

"Chaucer! Back away! That is not a dog! That's a raccoon! He might have rabies!"

Might was being optimistic. The animal had open wounds on its legs and neck. It salivated and looked deranged.

Chaucer's leash dragged behind him.

I picked up a second smaller tree branch and considered my options.

There weren't many.

I threw the smaller piece of wood to the side. My hope was that one of them would go after it. Chaucer might think I was playing fetch with him. I had no understanding of raccoon psychology, but maybe he would think the stick was food.

Neither one fell for the stick trick.

The smoke grew thicker behind me. I could even feel heat. I glanced over my shoulder to see that the fire had really taken off. The flames licked the vegetation where Chaucer and I had slept the night before.

I threw the larger limb into the shrubs behind the agitated raccoon. This time the raccoon was interested.

When he turned to look at the stick, I snagged Chaucer's leash and pulled him away. We ran toward the expanding fire. I grabbed my backpack and dragged Chaucer to the place on the island farthest from both the fire and the raccoon.

43

HANNAH

E xpeditious *(adj.) done with speed and efficiency*

DAD, Corker and I stood in the parking lot of the boatyard and talked.

Corker's phone rang. As he stepped away to talk, Katelyn and her dad pulled up in his pickup.

"Hey, Hannah," Katelyn said, rolling down her window.

"Hey," I said, then glanced past her to her dad. "Hi, Mr. Calhoun."

He waved, and both of them looked at me expectantly.

"Oh, sorry." I motioned to Dad. "This is my dad, John Simmons."

I recognized the expression on their faces. I'd seen it almost every time one of my friends, their parents, or even a teacher met Dad for the first time. Silently, they were pondering whether I was adopted or if they'd missed the clues that I wasn't as white as they'd thought. It would almost be funny if it didn't hurt so much to see my dad's shoulders slump each time it happened.

"Oh," Katelyn said. "Um, nice to meet you, Mr. Simmons."

"You, too," Dad said. "Hannah's told us all about you."

Mr. Calhoun pointed toward the shop. "We were just on our way to the shop to grab a tool I need at home."

I nodded. "Well, see you at school on Tuesday."

"Yeah," Katelyn said. "Bye."

"Hey, wait!" I said. "You haven't seen Hank, have you?"

"No. Why?"

"Just wondering," I answered.

"Sorry," Katelyn said. "See you Tuesday." They drove toward the boat shop.

Officer Corker came back and addressed Dad. "A Florida state trooper pulled over a pickup towing your boat on I-95, near Jacksonville, Florida. The driver's license says James Madison from Idaho. It appears to be fake and so is the plate. He's in custody, and your boat is with the Florida state police," Corker said. "They're running his prints, so we'll have an ID on him soon."

Dad nodded. "That's good."

"Can we all agree that Emmitt is up to no good?" I asked.

Dad shrugged. "I'm suspicious of the guy, and I've never even met him."

"He lied to Brock about why they were moving boats around on the dry stacks. Why lie—unless you have something to hide?" I said. "He left his keys in his truck, and the thieves used it to move our boat to the ramp so they could steal it." I scoffed. "The guy stole gas from his father in the middle of the night and loaded it onto a boat that wasn't his. The day before the burglary, Rodney Buckley was at his house. The following day, Rodney rented the trailer and container that was seen at the boatyard before the robbery but was gone after the robbery."

"We don't know for sure that the truck Rodney rented was used in the burglary," Corker said.

Always a stickler.

"What about the fact that Emmitt knew about Hugo biting

someone at the boat ramp?" I looked at Corker. "When will you get the results back from the fur testing?"

"Uh... I... uh... never sent that off," Corker mumbled.

"What? You promised! Whoever that dog bit was probably one of the thieves!"

"Hannah," Corker shuffled his feet in the gravel. "Buckley practically bankrupted the police department. I *told* Hank I didn't have money for DNA testing. I just said I'd send it off to appease him."

"Well, I guess we'll never know who the dog bit, then!"

I grabbed my father's hand. "Let's go, Dad!"

44

HANK

*A*n accelerant is any substance that speeds the development or growth of fire. Accelerants are frequently used to commit arson, and some accelerants may cause an explosion. Gasoline is the most common accelerant. See Forensics 411 episode 43, "Burning for You," for more information.

I LED Chaucer to the edge of the water facing the mainland then turned to watch the flames engulf the island.

"Smokey is not going to be happy about this!" I told Chaucer.

We watched more previously wet foliage catch fire.

I rubbed Chaucer's head, using him as the comfort object that he was, and had always been. We're going to need to build a bunker."

I dug in the sand with my hands. When Chaucer saw what I was doing, he joined in, digging alongside me.

"That's a good boy." I tried to keep a calm tone for Chaucer's sake. "We can sit down low to get away from the smoke. I don't want to go in the water unless we absolutely have to."

We scooped sand frantically while the campfire grew from bonfire to wildfire, swallowing the shrubs and trees. The smoke I had wanted earlier floated in our direction and burned my eyes. "If nobody noticed our fire before, they sure will now," I told Chaucer with a cough.

He just kept digging. It was a job he took seriously.

"Okay, Buddy, that's enough. You'll hurt your paws, like when you found Stacy's body. You rest. All we can do now is wait. Someone will see the fire or smell the smoke. We'll stay low and breathe the clean air coming off the water."

I slumped against the sand wall and watched Chaucer rub his eyes with his paws. "If you close your eyes, the smoke won't burn as much."

Like the perfect dog he was, Chaucer lay down, closed his eyes, and rested his chin on his front legs. I stroked his ears, then moved my hands around his body, searching for wounds from his battle with the raccoon.

"What's this, Buddy?" I pulled my hand away from something sticky on the skin folds of his neck and held it to the fire light.

"Blood." My heart sank.

I'd done it again. Chaucer was hurt, and it was my fault. I punched my thigh with the side of my fist. "You just can't help yourself, can you? Every chance you get, you manage to put Chaucer in danger! Now he's probably got rabies, and here you are," my voice cracked, "stranded on this stupid island that's about to burn up!"

As if in response to my carelessness and stupidity, something exploded. The island belched a thundering boom and spit flaming branches and sand into the air.

By instinct, I ducked and covered my head, but Chaucer— driven by his own instinct—leapt into the water and yelped, his leash dragging behind him.

"No, Chaucer! You'll get cut!"

I tried to reach his leash, but with just one step into the water, I felt the slicing sensation of an oyster shell on the bottom of my foot.

"Ow! Freaking oysters!" I called to Chaucer, "Come closer. Come on, boy! Closer. This way." I stretched my body to its full length and swiped the water, trying to make contact with the sinking leash.

The pain registered in his frightened eyes as he attempted to obey my command and inch back toward me. With each step, he yelped, cried... whimpered.

"I know, boy. It hurts. That's why we didn't try this earlier." I extended my arms even farther. "It's okay. I've got you."

My hand grasped the leash and I dragged him back onto the sand as he protested every step across the lacerating oyster shells.

Out of breath, I collapsed into our sand bunker and inspected our feet. Chaucer's were worse than mine, but we were both pretty cut up.

"Come here, lay down."

I took the plastic bowl from my backpack, scooped water from the marsh, and poured it over Chaucer's paws.

He whined.

"I know boy. This water's not the cleanest, but I need to get the mud out of your cuts."

He jumped up, tugging hard toward the water.

I yanked him down forcefully, then threw my weight on top of him. Behind us, the island burned.

45

HANNAH

A *ppease (v.) placate someone by giving into their demands*

"HANNAH?" Mom knocked on the door at about nine that night. "Hank's mom just called. The Coast Guard found him and Chaucer. He's at the hospital in Wilmington."

"The hospital?"

"Yes."

She considered me for a long moment, then said, "I can take you to see him."

"Really? You'll take me?"

"Yes."

I jumped off my bed and wrapped my arms around her. "Thank you, Mom!"

MOM STAYED in the waiting room while I went to see Hank. His "room" was a curtain-walled cubicle, with other patients a few steps away in their own curtained areas. His grandpa and mom smiled at me when I peeked in, then stood up.

"We'll be back in a few."

I sat where Hank's mom had been, next to the hospital bed.

"What happened?" I asked.

"I went south on the waterway and found the pontoon boat beached on a saltmarsh island. The jon boat was gone. A guy had been camping on the island and was packing up when we got there. He took off on the pontoon boat. I'd hidden *Crime Cat* in a cove and, while Chaucer and I were investigating, I think the guy in the pontoon spotted my boat and took it."

"And your cell phone was on the boat," I said. "The Coast Guard found it in the river."

He nodded. "The guy must've found it and chucked it. It was probably ringing off the hook once Mom figured out I was gone. The Coast Guard took Chaucer to Doc Taylor's clinic. He has to get some shots and be quarantined for a few days because of a run-in with a possibly rabid raccoon. He cut up his paws really bad on the oysters, and tons of bacteria live in those things."

"Aww. His poor paws. Again!" I examined Hank's bandaged feet.

He explained how he started the fire. "I think it was my can of bug spray that exploded. Someone must've heard it, or they saw the fire, and called 911. The EMS just brought me here to check me for smoke inhalation, clean my cuts, and give me a tetanus shot and some antibiotics."

"Gosh, I'm glad you're okay."

I let my pinky touch his.

He smiled at me and put three of his fingers on my hand.

"I couldn't tell who was on the pontoon boat," he said, "but I don't think it was Emmitt. The guy started both the pontoon's engines and seemed genuinely surprised at how loud they were. Emmitt already knew that using both engines was noisy. It must've been someone else. I'm going with the theory that

Emmitt delivered the pontoon to that person on the island, then left in the jon boat."

"Hacktivist77 sent me the security footage from Monday. Guess who paid a visit to Coastal Freight Logistics?"

"Who?"

"Rodney Buckley!" I said. "Roy Buck Denley is an anagram for Rodney Buckley! He rented the red eighteen-wheeler! Officer Cantrell verified it."

I explained about the list of slip numbers I'd found in the forklift, and the marina security footage of someone filling up the gas cans, and everything Brock and Mr. Fripp said. "And the cops found our boat in Florida!"

"That's great!"

"Neither Brock nor Mr. Fripp knew anything about the pontoon, but they said Emmitt owns a jon boat."

Hank rubbed his arms that were covered in scratches.

"Nobody's seen Emmitt since about eight o'clock on Saturday evening—well, except for us. Brock and Mr. Fripp said he scheduled today off weeks ago. Both have been trying to call him," I said. "Brock did tell us that Rodney, of all people, was over at their house on Sunday evening before the robbery and that he and Emmitt went out in the yard to talk. Apparently, they've been friends since high school."

"Interesting," Hank said. "I think it's obvious that Rodney and Emmitt were somehow involved in the robbery. The question is, how deep into it are they?"

"Don't you think Brock would've noticed if Emmitt left their house in the middle of the night Monday?" I said. "Besides, he would've had to take Brock's truck since his was at the boatyard."

"Rodney could've picked Emmitt up, so he could participate in the robbery." Hank said. "We need to find out what kind of car Rodney drives and see if it showed up on Eugene Lund's video doorbell."

"Marcia Masters already checked on that. Rodney doesn't have a car registered to his name, and his license is suspended for driving without insurance. I think Marcia was supposed to research the owners of each of the cars on the video, *if* Corker actually asked her to do it."

"What do you mean, *if*?"

"He never sent the dog fur off for DNA testing!"

"What?"

"He only *said* he was going to do it to appease you."

"Jeez! What is his problem?" Hank ran a hand through his hair. "Do the Florida cops know the name of the person who had your boat?"

"Yes. His name is James Madison."

"James Madison?" Hank said. "As in President James Madison?"

"The Florida cops think it's an alias."

"Do you have your phone?" Hank asked.

"My mom locked it in our family safe." I scoffed. "I didn't even know we had a family safe! I got two months with no phone, no allowance, and I'm grounded. I'm not even allowed to take driver's ed this semester!"

"But your mom let you come here?"

"She actually brought me. I suspect Dad injected her with an elephant tranquilizer."

"Wouldn't Rodney have needed a driver's license to rent the flatbed truck?"

"Yes, he used Roy Buck Denley's license. It was fake."

"Yep." Hank said. "We need Corker to get the cigarette butts and dog fur tested so we know who we're looking for. I bet whoever they are, they're in Florida."

Hank's mom came back in. "Sweetie, they said you can go home."

"Great!"

"Um, I don't know when I'll get to talk to you again since I'm incarcerated and all," I said.

"Oh, trust me," Ms. Boyd said, "you're not the only one who's going to be doing time."

I gave Hank's hand a squeeze. "Talk to you in a couple months."

46

HANK

The National Institute of Justice published a study saying law enforcement agencies were five times more likely to identify a suspect with DNA evidence than with fingerprints alone. They also found that blood evidence was more effective in solving crimes than other biological evidence left behind when items were touched by the suspect. For more details, see Forensics 411 episode 13, "Looking for Clues."

WHEN WE ARRIVED BACK HOME that night, Mom said, "Go sleep. We will be having a long discussion in the morning."

I showered off the smoke smell and collapsed into bed, hoping Chaucer was sleeping comfortably at Doc Taylor's.

THE NEXT DAY was Labor Day. I didn't have to go to school, and Mom didn't have to go to work. With a full day of lecturing opportunity at her disposal, she took her time handing down my sentence.

She didn't even come in my room until noon.

When she did, she positioned herself on the bed and appeared to be choosing her words carefully. "I'm glad you enjoy forensics. I think it's fine that you make videos and blog about crime. What bothers me is when you are in danger, put Hannah in danger, or flat out break the law. I also don't like Hannah sneaking into your bedroom, or the two of you sneaking out of the house," she said. "I have enough to deal with, with Dad's dementia, especially now that we know he's been wandering off. I can't lie awake at night and worry whether you're in bed or not."

I swallowed hard.

"You are grounded for two months," she continued. "I will replace your cell phone because I still worry about you constantly after what happened in sixth grade. I want you home immediately after school. I'm going to take Dad to the senior citizen center every day on my way to work. They have a van to give him a ride home at four o'clock, and you will be here to keep an eye on him."

I nodded.

"I broke up with Steve."

If she was waiting for an *I'm sorry to hear that*, it wasn't going to happen.

"He's an adult and should know better than to allow you into investigations. I told him I didn't want you involved in the robbery case, and he let you in, anyway. He had to know you'd do something impulsive and stupid."

I sat up straighter.

"What do you mean 'impulsive and stupid'? Steve is incompetent!"

"He's not incompetent. He's just been overwhelmed trying to clean up the mess Chief Buckley left. Besides, I don't care whether he's Barney Fife or Sherlock Holmes. I care about you and your safety."

"The only thing we did wrong was sneaking out at night to go to the marina."

Mom stood up. "No! No! No! That's not the only thing you did wrong! Kids doing police work is dangerous! And it's where I draw the line."

"But Mom—we're so close to solving this case. We just need the results of the DNA tests on the cigarettes and dog fur, and we'll know who we're looking for."

"*We* don't need anything. The police will handle it."

47

HANNAH
TUESDAY

S *alient (adj.) most notable or important*

HANK WAS at the bus stop ten minutes early. I knew that because I arrived eleven minutes early.

"I think you have a very legitimate excuse to stay home today," I said. "We don't want you foaming at the mouth in second period."

"Get it all out of your system," he said, "because you are not going to mention anything about it to anyone. So, go on—hit me with your best shot."

"Speaking of shots…" I stomped my foot. "No! It's no fun if you give me permission!"

"Do you think Corker actually sent the fur and cigarette butts to the crime lab this time?"

Hank shrugged. "Who knows? What's most important is that Mom broke up with him."

"Really? That's too bad."

"No, it's good," he said. "If you ever write my parents' love story, like you said, there is no way on earth it should end with her being with the Casanova Cop."

"He's not *that* bad," I said. "But it would be a little anti-climactic."

"More like a Shakespearean tragedy," he said.

I shrugged. "Hey, the other night at the hospital, you asked if I had my phone. Did you want me to look up something about James Madison?" I flashed a smile. "Because I did!"

"Business cards!" he said. "You're just trying to get your name on the top of the card at this point, aren't you?"

"Maybe." I flashed him a coy smile.

"If someone chooses the name James Madison as an alias, there's a reason."

"Another anagram?" I said.

"I doubt it," Hank said, "This person who calls himself James Madison had your boat, so he is either one of the thieves or he got it from the thieves."

"The Florida police were running his prints."

"They should have a name by now," Hank said. "Tell me what you found out about James Madison."

I had practically memorized the articles I'd read. "He was one of the authors of the *Federalist Papers,* which were a bunch of essays written around 1789. They were designed to convince US citizens to ratify the Constitution after the Articles of Confederation had failed spectacularly. He was also president during the War of 1812. That's sometimes called the *Second American Revolution* because, even after we got our independence from England, they didn't really respect us as a sovereign nation."

"Didn't Madison have something to do with the second amendment?" Hank asked.

"He proposed it."

We heard the bus's squealing brakes a few streets away.

"And that's the one that allows militias to have guns to protect themselves in the event that the government tries to get too powerful, right?"

At that moment, our bus pulled up.

We fought through the shoulders to an empty seat in the middle. It was the one above the wheel that had absolutely no leg room, but it was almost always available. Hank called it the black jellybean of bus seats. If there was anything that most people rejected, he called it a *black jellybean*. I personally liked the black ones.

"When we get to school, go in the office and ask if you can use the phone. That's how kids had to call people from school in the olden days."

I grunted. "I guess I'm going to have to get used to the dark ages. Are we going to have to make a tin-can phone? I really don't understand the science behind that."

"I'm supposed to get my new phone today, and you still have your tablet and laptop, so we can email each other or Snapchat."

As we went in the building, I asked, "Who am I calling?"

"Corker. Since Mom dumped him, you need to be the middle-man."

"What am I asking him?"

"Whether he took the samples for DNA testing, and when he will get the results back," Hank said. "Also, whether he's found Emmitt or Rodney, and does he know James Madison's real identity."

Using Corker's business card, I made the call while Hank waited on the green vinyl couch in the office.

I reported back. "Corker said he personally delivered the samples to the regional crime lab in Jacksonville yesterday and asked the staff to put a rush on it. He might have the names of the cigarette smokers tomorrow. He hasn't found Rodney or Emmitt, and he told me to tell you to quit making me do your dirty work!"

"Shoot!" Hank snapped his fingers. "I wanted you to ask Corker where James Madison's driver's license was from."

"Oh," I said, "I know that. James Madison hails from the Gem State."

"The Gem State? Where's that?"

"Idaho," I said. "Same place Roy Buck Denley got his driver's license."

48

HANK

The Miami area police collected DNA from 526 burglaries in which they had no suspect. After running those DNA profiles through the Combined DNA Index System (CODIS), they were able to match 271 of the samples to a previously convicted criminal. In other words, very few criminals only strike once, and recovering DNA evidence at a "lesser" crime like a burglary or drug bust has helped solve other burglaries as well as violent crimes. For more information, see Forensics 411 *episode 26, "Double Trouble for Suspects."*

IN FIRST PERIOD, Mrs. Ozmore was walking between rows, handing out books.

"We're going to begin reading a memoir today. The author grew up in a fundamentalist Mormon family in Idaho without any formal education and quite an unusual family life because her father was a prepper."

"Don't you mean *preppy*, Mrs. Ozmore?" some girl asked.

"No," our teacher answered while continuing to place a book on each desk. "The author's father was, actually still *is*, a doomsday prepper. He's spent a large part of his life preparing for impending disaster. It could be a natural disaster, an interruption in services like electricity or water, a civil war, or even a global catastrophe. When the you-know-what hits the fan, the prepper's goal is to survive by being self-sufficient. Sometimes they're called survivalists."

"Why," the girl asked, "would *anyone* want to survive the end of the world?"

I stared at the cover.

Idaho.

One of the least populated states in the US. A state out there in the middle of nowhere. A state known for... what... potatoes?... and apparently gems.

It was also where Rodney Buckley used to live as part of a survivalist group! The *Vista Point Voice* had interviewed him about it a few years back when he still talked.

"Mrs. Ozmore, I think I'm gonna be sick!" I ran out of the room, thereby perpetuating the rumor that I had gastrointestinal issues.

But instead of going to the bathroom, I ran to the media center.

At a computer, I typed "Second American Revolution, preppers" in the search bar. The first couple of hits were articles about the War of 1812, but the third link was titled, "Preppers, Survivalists Say Another American Revolution Coming Soon."

The article explained how fringe militia groups are preparing for a revolution against our government that they feel no longer represents its citizens. One group, the Madison Militia, headquartered in northern Idaho, is suspected to fund its stockpile of weapons, food, and fuel through criminal activity.

"May I use your phone?" I asked the media specialist.

"Don't you have your own?"

"No."

"Really?" She seemed genuinely shocked and borderline hostile.

"Really," I said.

"Okay, fine. You have to dial nine first."

I called Corker.

"It's Hank. Rodney Buckley is the thread that ties all the pieces of the robbery together! He used to live in a survivalist compound out in Idaho. He used a fake license from Idaho when he rented the tractor-trailer from Coastal Freight. The guy, James Madison, that the cops pulled over with Hannah's boat, had an *Idaho* license." I took a breath and rushed on. "Think about it, if you were making a fake driver's license, would *Idaho* be the first state that popped in your head? No. It's one of those states that people on the east coast forget even exists... unless you have a connection to it. I bet the thieves are people Rodney met when he was living at the survivalist compound in Idaho."

Corker seemed to take a moment to process all of that, then responded. "The Florida State Troopers identified the guy with the Simmons's boat as Leroy Delco, and he actually *is* from Idaho. He has a long record of larceny, domestic abuse and weapons violations. He's known to be part of a militia group, and he's not talking."

"Does he have a dog bite on his hand?" I asked.

"As a matter of fact, the state troopers said his hand is bandaged," Corker said. "Delco wouldn't say what happened, but the Florida authorities said it could be a dog bite."

I rolled my eyes at the telephone. We could've tied Leroy Delco to the robbery days earlier if Corker had sent off the blood-stained dog fur to be tested when I gave it to him.

"Ask the Florida authorities to take photos of the hand. We can see if it matches Hugo's dental pattern."

"Hang on," Corker said, "I've got another call."

I sat on hold for about sixty seconds.

"That was the crime lab," Corker said. "The blood on the fur belongs to Leroy Delco."

I let the news hang there between us while I waited for him to say *you were right*.

"Look, I'm sorry. I should've sent that sample off for testing when you suggested it."

"What about the cigarette butts?" I said.

"The cigarettes were smoked by two different people: Colton Eubanks and Raphael Jones, both from Florida."

"I bet those two are connected to a militia group, doomsday preppers, or have experience getting stolen goods over to the Caribbean," I said. "Maybe all three. You have the resources. Dig. I bet you'll find that Leroy Delco and Rodney Buckley know each other. In fact, I wouldn't be surprised if our international theft ring is homegrown right here in America!"

Corker didn't respond.

"And I also bet that every single one of them has previous arrests. They would've been on your radar earlier if you'd just run the DNA tests." I couldn't resist saying it out loud.

"You're right, I'm wrong." Corker cleared his throat.

"I'm at school. I don't have a cell phone right now, but I'd like you to keep me informed."

"You know I can't do that. Your mom said *no more.*"

"You just told me about Leroy Delco. The lab confirmed that that blood on the dog fur was important. The cigarette butts were important. Face it, every break you've gotten in this case is because of me or Hannah. You need us."

"Yes. You two are the wonder twins," Corker said. "I've got APBs out for the red tractor trailer, Emmitt, Rodney, and I'm adding Leroy Delco, Colton Eubanks, and Raphael Jones to the list."

"And while you're waiting for someone to spot them, all the stolen goods could be half-way to the Bahamas."

"I've got everything under control," Corker said.

"Uh-huh." I hung up without even bothering to say goodbye.

"Thank you," I said to the media specialist, who must've been eavesdropping on my conversation because she was giving me one of those *I find what you said interesting* looks that Dr. Blanchard was always telling me to fake.

Instead of going back to English class, I marched straight out the front door of the school.

I had a hunch.

49

HANNAH

E **ntitled** *(adj.) believing oneself to be inherently deserving of privileges or special treatment*

FIRST PERIOD, supposedly math class, might as well be known as Madison class. Every day, the teacher spent a large portion of the period waiting for Madison T to turn around, stop talking, put her nail polish away, put her phone away, *et cetera*. As my mom would say, Madison T was a *handful*.

Now, she was in front of me in the hall as we all shifted from first to second period.

Yay me!

"If you want, I can get you one just like it," she said to Madysen H.

"I don't have any money," Madysen H said, "especially for something from Blue Moon. That place is so expensive."

"I told you, I get the five-finger discount when Kelsey is working."

Madysen H touched Madison T's scarf. "Do they have it in a peach color?"

"If they don't have peach, what's your second choice?"

"Dark blue," Madysen H said. "Are you sure we won't get in trouble?"

"Positive. I got these earrings there, too. And Lexi's bracelet, have you seen it?"

"Okay," Madysen H said. "Get me a scarf like that."

Five finger discount! I knew what that meant. Madison T had a bad and very *illegal* hobby.

50

HANK

*A*n accessory-after-the-fact *is a person who assists someone who has committed a crime* after *the crime was committed — with knowledge that the person committed the crime, and with the intent to help the person avoid punishment.* See Forensics 411 *episode 22, "Talk the Talk."*

A MILE. That's how far I jogged from the school to Gravely Street, where the Fripp brothers shared a house. I didn't know their address, but based on what Hannah said, I knew they had a dog they kept in the back yard.

Gravely Street had seven houses. Steve lived in the last house on the right, leaving six I didn't know. And only three had fenced yards.

I opened the mailbox of the first house with a fenced yard. The mail hadn't come yet, so no clues there.

I decided to take the direct route and ring the doorbell. An older lady answered the door.

"Hello, ma'am. I'm looking for Emmitt and Brock Fripp's house. Do you know which one it is?"

"It's one oh six."

"Thank you, ma' am."

The Fripp brothers lived in a small beige house like Corker's. It was probably eighty years old. Set back in some pine trees, it didn't have grass growing in the yard and needed a lot of TLC.

The dog barked at me as I marched up the driveway. I went to the gate and let him sniff my hand. "It's okay, boy," I said. "I work for the police."

To the left, a door slammed shut, and I saw Emmitt, barefoot, running for the woods.

Rather than chase him, I slipped into the house and used Emmitt's flip phone, sitting on the kitchen counter, to call Corker.

"Never underestimate the bond between twins," I said to him.

"What are you talking about?" He didn't seem to notice I'd called from a different number.

"I'm at Emmitt and Brock's house. Emmitt just took off into the woods behind his house. He lives down the street from you. He's been right under your nose."

Corker cussed like I'd never heard him cuss before. "I'm on my way. Just do me a favor and stay there at his house. I don't want you getting in any more trouble."

AN HOUR LATER, Corker pulled into the Fripp's driveway with Emmitt in the back seat.

"Hop in," Corker said. "I'm taking you back to school."

I climbed in the front seat. "Seriously? I hand you Emmitt, and you're going to send me back to suffer through a school lunch?"

"Yes!" Corker scowled at me. "I'm tired of being manipulated by you."

"Fine." I turned to Emmitt behind the glass divider. "Did Brock know where you were all along?"

Emmitt shrugged.

"That would make him an accomplice. Was Brock in on it? Are your parents going to get to visit two kids in jail, or just one?"

"Brock doesn't know anything!" Emmitt said. "You leave him out of this!"

"Why'd you do it?" I asked. "I can't imagine your dad was in on it because you've basically destroyed his business with your little scheme."

"Leave him alone," Corker said. "Save it for when we get to the station house, Emmitt!"

I didn't give up. "You ruined the business your dad spent forty years building."

I stared at him and waited. When you present a person with silence, they usually feel the need to fill it.

Emmitt obliged. "You think this is how it was supposed to turn out?" His voice shook. "I was just trying to help Pop. He invested everything he had to build the stacks, and now he's going to lose the whole marina. He hasn't been able to make a single payment. Rodney said he had some friends who could help us out. All I had to do was let them into the boatyard to look at our storage inventory."

"So, someone came, checked out all the boats, made a list of which boats they liked, and you just had to make sure they were on the bottom row the night of the robbery," I said.

He shifted in the seat. "Rodney said Pop wouldn't be out anything because his buddies would only steal stuff from other people's boats. Just about everybody has insurance on their boats, so no one would get hurt."

"How much did they pay you?"

"Eighty-thousand." His voice cracked. "But I wasn't gonna keep it. I was going to give it to Pop."

"And Rodney got some sort of finder's fee, right?" I said.

He shrugged.

"When did you tell Brock what was going on?"

"Leave him out of this. He didn't know anything!"

I took a stab in the dark. "I suspect Brock's been hiding you since you came home after delivering the pontoon boat to Rodney on the marsh island."

Emmitt scoffed.

The police radio squawked, and Corker fiddled with it.

"I followed you that night. I saw Rodney leave the island on the pontoon boat loaded up with gas cans," I said, not letting on I was guessing that Rodney was the mystery man. "That's so he wouldn't have to stop at a marina to fill up until he was far from here, right? He's traveling by water and headed to Florida, isn't he? That's where he's going to meet up with Leroy Delco, Raphael Jones, and Colton Eubanks. Leroy was the one with the dog bite. Did you know their names?"

I turned a bit more in my seat for a better look at Emmitt. "Did you know the Florida State Troopers arrested your friend, Leroy Delco?" I asked, hoping to push him over the edge. "Or do you call him James Madison?"

Emmitt glared at me.

"Leroy showed up in Florida towing the Sea Runner that belongs to my friend's family. Somebody used your truck to put that boat in the water, then drove it to Georgia. There, someone else, or maybe the same person, pulled it out of the water, loaded it on a trailer, and Leroy Delco was in the process of delivering it to Florida—or was he just going to keep it for himself?"

"I don't know anything about that," Emmitt said as we pulled into the school parking lot.

I leaned toward Corker. "Do you have enough to go on?" I whispered. "Find the red truck. I'd say it's in Florida. The thieves are most likely somewhere remote because they have the skills to live off the land. Check the Everglades. "

Corker studied me with an expression I couldn't interpret. Non-verbal communication wasn't my strong suit, but I had a feeling that even Corker didn't know what he was feeling. Gratitude for my help? Anger at my interference? Humiliation for his failures?

"Go to class, and neither one of us is going to mention this to your mother."

"Got it!" I said, getting out of the car. I came around to the driver's side, leaned in the front window, slipped Emmitt's flip phone to Corker, and whispered, "I have a strong suspicion this phone will put you in contact with the thieves. Use it wisely."

"Um, thanks," Corker said.

I looked at Emmitt. "You're best off just spilling the beans. Don't try to protect Rodney or Leroy or any of the others 'cause they're not gonna have your back. They may cover for each other, but you're an outsider. You were just a means to an end."

I gave him a salute and jogged in the school building.

51

HANNAH

*S**hoplifting** (n.) the criminal action of stealing goods from a store while pretending to be a customer*

"WHERE WERE YOU DURING SECOND PERIOD?" I asked Hank when I flopped down next to him at lunch with my tray of inedibles and undesirables.

"I had to go find Emmitt. Turns out he was at his house."

"Hannah told me about your suspicions involving Emmitt Fripp. I just can't believe he would rob his own father!" Katelyn said.

"Your dad said Emmitt and Brock had always been inseparable. When you're in trouble, who can you trust more than your own twin?" Hank said.

"So," I said, "on Sunday when Brock said he hadn't heard from Emmitt, was he lying?"

"I don't know. But Brock figured it out whenever Emmitt came home." Hank pushed something brown around on his tray. "I don't think Emmitt actually knows all the thieves. Maybe he doesn't know *any* of them, but he knew one of them was bitten by Hugo the German Shepherd."

"Who's Hugo?" Katelyn asked.

I explained how we met Hugo and gave the bloody fur sample to Corker.

Katelyn seemed mad for not being included.

"You had band practice when we met first met Hugo, and you were at the mall the day we confirmed that he had bitten someone," Hank said. "I texted you."

She blushed. "The mall's fun."

"And he confirmed that Rodney Buckley was the go-between that set up the robbery," Hank continued. "*Maybe* he was one of the thieves. Maybe not. I'm not even sure if Emmitt knows where Rodney is right now. But I really believe it was Rodney that Emmitt delivered the pontoon boat to."

I picked up a limp French fry, studied it, then changed my mind.

"Several of the suspects have ties to an Idaho militia group," Hank said, "and Rodney lived out there in one of those prepper groups for a while. Emmitt said his take from the robbery was eighty thousand and he only did it to help his father. Old Man Fripp mortgaged everything to build those stacks but couldn't make the payments."

Katelyn nodded. "My dad said he had only rented out about half the slips in the dry stacks, so he probably wasn't bringing in enough money to cover his expenses."

"Emmitt ended up hurting his dad and his business." Hank concluded his wrap-up of his morning escapades.

"Is Corker going to keep you informed about what happens?" I asked.

"He said he couldn't because he had promised Mom, but then he told me a bunch of things he probably shouldn't have. He's easy to trip up."

"Well, maybe we can pry some information out of him later. I have a name of a suspect in the shoplifting that's been going on downtown."

"Really?" Hank said.

"I overheard Madison T talking about how she could get things for free whenever someone named Kelsey was working. She was going to go after school to steal a scarf for Madysen H."

"She has a sister named Kelsey," Katelyn said. "She's a senior and works at a little boutique on Main Street."

"Blue Moon?" I asked.

"Yeah."

"Can I use your cell phone, Katelyn?" Hannah said.

"What happened to yours?"

"I'm grounded. No phone. No driver's ed. No fun."

"What did you do?" she asked.

I glanced at Hank, and he turned away to hide his tiny smirk. "Nothing really. Just some extreme parenting from Jen and John."

"Call the main non-emergency number and ask for Cantrell instead of Corker," Hank said. "We're going to need to make a new friend in the Vista Point police department."

52

HANK

S hoplifting is the number one property crime in the United States. More than $13 billion in merchandise is stolen from retailers each year. Twenty-five percent of shoplifters are under eighteen years old. See Forensics 411 *episode 47, "Sticky Fingers," for more information about the consequences of shoplifting.*

MOM CAME home with my new phone. Every parental tracking device on the planet was installed on it. She could probably monitor my heartrate from her desk at work.

I emailed Hannah to tell her I had my new phone and a new number. I liked to get a new number about once a year to keep Dillon guessing.

She emailed back: Go to Snap so we can talk.

I sent a thumbs up.

Hannah: Did you see the news? 4 suspects arrested in the boatyard robbery.

I wrote back: Emmitt, Leroy Delco? Who else?

Hannah: Colton Eubanks and Raphael Jones found in Florida with almost 3 million in stolen boat engines and electronics.

I sent her another thumbs up.

She asked about Chaucer, we speculated on whether Cantrell had arrested Madison Talbot for shoplifting, then said goodbye.

As I exited Snapchat, I saw that I had an email from *MyDNAHistory.com.*

I opened the email and read: `Congratulations Henry Adam Boyd!`—I'd used *Adam* on the form before I knew any better—`You have a new DNA relative. We predict that Sitara Zalmai is your first cousin.`

ACKNOWLEDGMENTS

For Todd, Simon, and Henry, who made me a "boy mom" and all that comes with it. Many thanks to my readers who found something special in Vista Point and came back for another visit. Keep reading, there are more adventures to come. Finally, many thanks to Jodi Thompson at Fawkes Press and my editor, Twyla-Beth Lambert, for seeing something special in Hank, Hannah, and Chaucer.

To keep the stories coming, please consider the following:

- Leave a review on your favorite book site
- Tell a friend about *Forensics 411* and author Whitney Skeen
- Ask your local library to put Whitney's work on the shelf
- Recommend Fawkes Press books to your local bookstore
- Sign up for our First Looks & Freebies newsletter

Thanks for making great books possible!

WWW.WHITNEYSKEEN.COM
WWW.FAWKESPRESS.COM / NEWSLETTER

FAWKES PRESS